Lady Parker's Grand Affair

A Scandal in Surrey novel

Sandra Sookoo

Adventure. Humor. Inclusion. Romance

New Independence Books

LADY PARKER'S GRAND AFFAIR COPYRIGHT 2012 by Sandra Sookoo

Published by New Independence Books and Sandra Sookoo.
Digital ISBN: 9781502200082
Print ISBN: 9798201205195
Contact Information:
sandrasookoo@yahoo.com
newindepdencebooks@gmail.com
Visit me at sandrasookoo.com
Book Cover Design by Sandra Sookoo
Background: Deposit Photos
Heroine stock image: Period Images
Publishing History
First Digital Edition, 2012
Second Digital Edition, 2015
Third Digital Edition, 2018
Fourth Digital Edition, 2022
First Print Edition, 2022

Dedication

This book, as well as the series, wouldn't have been possible without the encouragement, dedication, support and patience of one person—Michele. Thanks so much. You'll never know just how much that means.

Author's Note

While this story is set at the end of the Regency time period, I'm of the opinion that both men and women in this era had the ability to be forward thinking and could have shown this in their actions as well. No one ever moves forward unless the status quo is challenged.

As such, I have taken a bit of literary license with my characters and the world in which they reside in the hopes that it will further bring this period to life with a bit of different perspective. Also, the stories in this series are a bit naughty with the appropriate matching words.

Chapter One

May 1820

Somewhere near Cranleigh, Surrey, England

Drat.

"Lady Parker, he's gaining on you!"

As her groom's warning rang in her ears, Margaret Parker leaned low over her horse's neck, the reins wound tight through her gloved fingers. She crooned encouragement to her mount. The mare's ears flicked as if in acknowledgement and her pace increased. The raw, equine power pulsed through every muscle in Maggie's body. She grinned. This was what living should feel like—the pound of her heartbeat, the strength of a mount between her thighs, the warmth of the afternoon sun beating down. Her green velvet skirts whipped about her legs. There was something to be said about riding astride. She had much more control over her horse than she would in a sidesaddle.

I intend to enjoy every second of doing what I please. Besides, it would give the local gentry something else to wag their tongues over. At least if they were gossiping about her, some other harassed female would get a brief reprieve.

"Don't worry, Billy. I see him!" She dug her heels into the ribs of her horse, willing the mare to run faster. The animal snorted. When she glanced over her shoulder to gauge the distance of her pursuer, the breeze caught the brim of her bonnet and blew it off her head. It thumped against her back, held at her throat by the satin ribbons.

Billy raced at her right. "Almost there, ma'am. Hold him off as best you can."

"I will." She wished to teach her brash, arrogant neighbor a thing or two about real women—and not the docile, English kind he thought all females should be.

On her left, and coming up strong, young Benjamin Chesley rode. She caught his flaming red hair out of the corner of her eye. The black legs of his magnificent stallion flashed into view as he nearly pulled abreast of her. She nudged her mount with her knee, praying for a bit more speed. The young man had scarcely turned sixteen, and needed to have his ego reined in. If she won the impromptu race, it would take some of the sass from him, and perhaps teach him not to underestimate women in general—and her in particular.

The end of the makeshift racecourse, a dirt path dotted with muddy puddles, loomed ahead. Benjamin's younger brother, Amos, jumped up and down, waving his arms, his red hair a burnished copper in the sun. A white cravat billowed from one hand. Maggie narrowed her eyes, bore down in the saddle with her knees clenched around the horse and slapped the reins. Her animal surged ahead of Benjamin's mount then left him altogether as she raced past Amos, grabbing the strip of cotton from the young man's hand.

Benjamin thundered past seconds later, shortly followed by Billy.

"Good show, Lady Parker!" Billy's shout of victory rang in her ears above the pounding of her pulse.

"Thank you, Billy. I never expected anything less." Maggie sat straight in the saddle and eased up on the reins. Her muscles quivered while she let her body relax. *Now that was an enjoyable way to pass the time, much better than stabbing my thumbs with the embroidery needle.* As she allowed her mare to cool down in a trot, she focused on Benjamin and resettled her skirts into a semblance of modesty. He'd wheeled his horse around and now faced her. "Well, Mr. Chesley, what have you to say now?" She tossed the cravat to Amos, having no further use for it.

A flush stained the youth's face scarlet. He pulled the brim of his cap low over his eyes and stared at his mount's ears. "I apologize, Lady Parker. Women are as accomplished as men."

Maggie set her bonnet back on her head and readjusted the ribbon beneath her chin. "And?" She lifted an eyebrow while her horse slowed to a walk.

His Adam's apple bobbed. "I have no cause to belittle the American spirit. England deserved every spanking they got in land and on sea."

"Very good."

The youth cleared his throat. "Do you want me to deliver Midnight to you tomorrow morning? He'll need to be fed, watered and brushed before I sign him over."

She bit her bottom lip to keep from laughing in the face of his defeat. "No, I think I've changed my mind. Even though your horse was my prize, I believe you've learned your lesson."

"Thank you, ma'am."

"I may not be so generous next time, so do keep my good will in mind." Maggie drew abreast of Benjamin. "I hope in the future you'll remember this race and school your thoughts accordingly." When he nodded, his gaze still downcast, she urged her mount into a faster walk. "Have a good day, gentlemen."

Grumbles reached her ears as she put distance between herself and the boys, followed by Amos's interjection, "That woman is quite mad. You should never have dared her to a race. She's deluded, besides. Men will always be better than women."

Benjamin shushed his brother as Maggie moved out of earshot. Billy followed at a more sedate pace.

She stroked her mare's neck, laughing when the horse tossed her head. "Mad? Not quite. Deluded? Not just yet, but at least I set tongues wagging, and I won't be forgotten." Unlike her departed husband, who no one ever remembered.

"Pardon, Lady Parker? Were you talking to me?" Concern hung on Billy's question.

"I was not. You'll grow into a fine young man someday."

"Thank you, ma'am. My ma sure hopes so. Tells me every morning to behave myself and do what my betters tell me."

"Your 'betters' are simply people with more money or popularity than you. Neither necessarily makes them better. Only a person's integrity can do that." If her dear father had instilled anything into her, it was that. Reputations could crumble like sugar in the rain, but honesty and integrity were made of stronger stuff. It was how you treated a person that mattered most.

"Yes, Lady Parker. My ma tells me that, too."

Familiar sadness welled in her chest. Jamie used to call her "ma" what seemed like an eternity ago now. Had it really been ten years since she'd lost him? Her heart squeezed in remembrance of his little hand clutching hers and the soft lilt of his laughter when something had pleased him. Those were the things that had comforted her when both Jamie and her husband were gone. *At least I had the experience. I cannot fault fate for that.*

A cloud of dust in the distance pulled her attention from her maudlin thoughts. She shaded her eyes as a rider approached. As he drew closer, she recognized the face and form of her brother Alfred Manning, and a smile parted her lips. "Billy." She twisted around. "Mr. Manning will accompany me home. You're free to return to your other duties, but thank you for the company."

"Thank you, ma'am, for the splendid race!" Billy clicked his tongue and his horse trotted down the lane.

Maggie tugged slightly on the reins. Her horse drifted to the side of the road, where it was content to munch on clumps of grass. As soon as her brother rode near, she hailed him with an exuberant wave. "Good afternoon, Alfie!"

He guided his mount near hers. "Must you continue to call me that ridiculous nickname?" His blue eyes, the exact shade of marble blue as hers, sparkled behind the lenses of his spectacles.

"It amuses me." Teasing Alfred was just one of the reasons she enjoyed having him around. While it was all well and good to bury herself in the country, away from the snobbery and waste of London, it also kept her away from the few relatives she did have in England. Alfred had been sent by her father to keep her company—which amounted to him either goading her into trouble or hauling her out of it.

She wiped at the perspiration on her brow with the back of her sleeve. "What brings you out? I thought you were busy meeting with the gardener?" As evidenced by his shirtsleeves rolled up to his elbows and his breeches splotched with dirt, Alfred, in his spare time, enjoyed categorizing the numerous plants, shrubs and flowers on the estate. His cravat, also smudged, hung at an awkward angle, as if he'd tried to adjust it before realizing his fingers were dirty.

"I was, and we were very much immersed in the rose garden, but Caruthers is about to have an apoplexy and sent me to find you. From the looks of things, you've gotten up to your usual mischief." He raked a hand through his dark brown hair, destroying the efforts his valet had put into setting it this morning.

Maggie smiled. "I have."

"At least you're enjoying yourself. It would seem your niece has arrived a day ahead of schedule and is even now sitting in the parlor awaiting your arrival."

A flutter of anticipation shot through her stomach. It had been an age since she'd last seen Amanda. "You are aware that Amanda is your niece as well?"

"Yes, but since I haven't spoken to our esteemed brother in years, I figure she's more yours than mine."

Maggie laughed. "Don't be jealous of Gregory. He cannot help that his services as an attorney are much in demand or that he can be rather a prick at times. I'm told New York is full of people needing a representative of the law, and he's good at it."

"At law or being a prick?"

She smiled, but didn't answer.

"Jealousy isn't in my nature" Alfred snorted. "Science might not be the popular choice, nor will it make me wealthy, but it interests me, and that is all that matters. I simply do not understand why Gregory allowed Amanda to make the trek not only to England, but from London down here to your Godforsaken estate."

"Remember, Amanda has been well-chaperoned. She's hardly been neglected."

"Yet she's come here. Are you her new nanny?" He guffawed as if it were some hysterical joke.

Perish the thought! "Ah, I can tell you why." Maggie didn't pull back on the reins as her horse drifted up the road to drink from a mud puddle. "Our dear niece has got it into her head that she'd enjoy living amidst the *Ton* for the Season, to see what all the fuss is about. Just turned eighteen, and with Gregory wrapped around her little finger, she wheedled the trip from him on one condition."

"And that would be?"

"That I sponsor her come out. He thinks the idea of Amanda attracting a titled gentleman is a good idea, and that it would be a great joke for an American girl to join the traditions of England. With Father's connections through the Navy, it was easy to secure invitations to balls and parties. However, I must accompany her, and fund the whole thing. After all, according to our dear brother, I'm sitting on piles of wealth with nothing to spend it on."

"Aren't you?" One of Alfred's eyebrows inched toward his hairline. "After all, your beloved Robert worked hard to petition the Crown to award you the barony with its entailment in the event of his premature passing and the birth of no further heirs."

"That he did." A pang of sadness gripped her. Despite her deceased husband's other faults, he'd been adamant about keeping the military title relevant, especially after they lost their son. Even now, it warmed her heart he'd seen potential in her, that she could do the title proud regardless of her being an American at heart. The longer she stayed in Surrey, the more her love of and loyalty to her property grew, as well as to its people if not England.

Alfred cleared his throat. "If you want my opinion, I think Amanda has seen the type of life you lead and the power you hold through the barony. She's trolling for exactly that."

"This might be true, brother dear, and I *am* sitting on a fortune, plus my dowry has earned decent interest, but I have numerous organizations, causes and people to give it to. A petulant adolescent who has done nothing to deserve the fortune is not on the agenda for handouts."

"You'll need to tread carefully."

"I will, but then, it is no one's business what I do with the money. Now that Robert is gone, I do what I please." Her smile slipped at the mention of her dead husband's name. "Good God, I didn't realize how much I hated his penny-pinching ways until just now."

She'd never had the latest gowns or shoes. According to Robert, if the garment was years old but still fit, there was no point in replacing it. After Jamie had been born, she'd never managed to lose the pregnancy weight and was unable to fit into her other clothes. That was the only time during their marriage Robert had conceded to buy her new gowns. Not to mention the years of only using four rooms in the manor because Robert wouldn't pay for coal to heat the whole structure. Oh, he'd kept her warm at night though. Maggie's smile wobbled. Despite his miserly ways, the dearly departed

Baron Parker had introduced her to pleasure in the bedroom, and for that she'd always be grateful and remember him fondly.

"But you've had eight years to do things your way and quite successfully at that." Alfred leaned over and patted her leg. "You've managed to flaunt convention like no one else I've seen and attained the rank of eccentric."

"I have. Though I hope, after everything, people will remember me fondly without whispered asides of how outrageous some of my antics have been." She urged her horse into a slow walk in the direction of the house.

His horse fell into step with hers. "Is there a reason you thumb your nose at society?"

"Perhaps." She couldn't contain her grin. "First and foremost, though I may reside in England now, I am an American. I think a society revolving around the titles and monetary worth of individuals is ridiculous, and any opportunity I have to laugh up my sleeve at the lot of them I'll take."

"That is readily obvious, my dear." Warm humor accompanied the statement.

"I may have married into the lowest rung of the peerage, but that doesn't mean two braces in the grand scheme. Since Robert's death, I've learned to live on my own, to figure out that being alone doesn't necessarily mean I need to be lonely." She waved a hand at the passing countryside, the rolling grasses, the lush trees and the stands of yellow and white wildflowers that dotted the landscape. "I could never enjoy the outdoors when Robert was alive. I used to joke that every living thing made him sneeze."

Companionable silence, broken only by the *clomp* of the horses' hooves against the earth, cropped up between them. Finally, Maggie sighed and glanced at her brother. "I sense you disagree with my viewpoint."

"I do, slightly." His smile softened the censure in his voice. "You've been by yourself for eight years, Mags. Are you sure you're happy living your unorthodox life?"

"Unorthodox how?"

He sighed, as it was a conversation they had many times. "Causing mischief through the countryside, or spending all your time alone. Have you ever considered marrying again? Giving me another niece or nephew?"

Another twinge of sadness squeezed her chest. "Oh bother. No doubt I'm too old to bear more children."

"You are just thirty-two. You are not a crone."

"No, but I'm quite firmly on the shelf and a widow besides."

Sometimes, in the quiet of the night, she'd lie in bed and imagine the musky smell of a masculine body clinging to the sheets, the feel of a man's arms around her, the insistent nudge of his cock or the sweet erotic bliss of love making. Her core throbbed. In the eight years since Robert's death, she'd never taken a lover, not even when the urge for coitus had nearly driven her out of her mind. In the daytime, she lived for her, but in the quiet of midnight, she missed having someone to share her experiences swith, having someone to talk to or with whom to share her joys and fears.

"Be honest, sis."

She willed the wayward desire to settle. "Marriage and childbearing made me vulnerable to a point. I don't know if I'm willing to offer my heart for more pain."

"I understand that, but nothing good in life comes without a certain risk."

Maggie swallowed around the lump in her throat. "I fear I'm too set in my ways to warrant interest from a gentleman. I was naïve when I married Robert, much like Amanda is. Now, I know more about life and what I want from it. I have a feeling most gentlemen won't want a woman who knows her own mind."

"Mags, is that really what you think? That has never held you back before. You were a wild girl. Marrying Robert stole some of your zest."

"Well—"

"Do you wish to stagnate here in the country and grow old without causing one great scandal that might launch your own coming out of sorts?"

Unexpected laughter burst from her throat. "What makes you think I haven't caused enough scandal around here already? Don't you remember the time I was caught swimming nude by the parson?" Her cheeks warmed. Oh, that had been hilariously ridiculous, being confined to the pond until she could convince the parson to move along after he'd prayed for her immortal soul.

Alfred's chuckle rang clear in the afternoon air. "What about the time you held the impromptu drinking contest at the local pub? You near drank everyone under the table."

"I did, much to the chagrin of the gray-haired dragons." Maggie laughed at that memory and the scoldings she'd received from everyone for a week afterward. "My, but the headache from the alcohol had me in bed for days."

Her brother's lips twitched. "I mean the big stories, the stuff gossips live for, the jaw-dropping *on dits* beyond the countrified gentry in Surrey."

"Such as?" Her heartbeat tripped fast as she waited.

He leaned closer. "An affair."

"Pardon me?"

"If you had done something along *those* lines, don't you think it would have reached London by now? Don't you think gawkers would angle for invitations to the estate for the sole purpose of seeing if you are the woman the tales said you were?"

"This is true. Maybe I haven't been nearly as naughty as I ought." Again, her thoughts fell to Robert and the fact no one in the area remembered him a year after his death. She shifted her focus to her father, the man of a thousand stories, the man of big exploits and bigger adventures, the man who loved his wife with a passion as fierce as his love of the Navy. Her heart ached. She'd not attained that level of commitment in her own marriage. How did she want to be remembered, because she most certainly didn't want to be forgotten?

"If flouting *London* society is your main goal, perhaps enacting a grand affair would gain you the attention you want and portray the story you are trying to tell. It might be just the thing to bring a worthy gentleman calling. Or..." The glance he slid her brimmed with mischief. "When you accompany Amanda to London, you could conduct your scandal there."

"Are you trying to have me ostracized from all of England, Alfie?" A thrill swept down her spine just the same. To have one grand affair, a dalliance with a rugged or charming gentleman, and then leave him happy, sated and pining. It was something she'd never attempted, but now that the idea had bloomed, she rather wanted to plan for it.

"No, I'm trying to secure your future happiness, and to remind you there is more to life than what you can find on these grounds—alone." His smile conveyed a smug attitude, even as he stared straight ahead. "You are too vibrant a woman to rusticate. I suspect you're only half-living, though you'd disagree with me. You need a man who can match you in temperament and daring, a man who won't give a fig if you're both caught swimming naked in the pond. At least give me something I can own and say 'Oh, *that* Margaret is my sister, and she is most certainly someone you need to meet.'"

His concern over her well-being sent humbling warmth through Maggie's body. "I'll bear your opinions in mind, but first, I need to take Amanda in hand. Gregory's last letter indicated she'd become rather trying with the frowns and attitude to match."

"Also, there is something else regarding dear Amanda."

Maggie narrowed her eyes as the rooftop of the manor house came into view. "Yes?"

"She hasn't come alone. A gentleman has accompanied her, along with your ancient nanny, of course."

Good Lord, she brought Nanny Beatrice? No doubt Gregory had contrived that. "Ah, she's already made a conquest, has she?" The knowledge made her smile. How lovely, Amanda would be an immediate success.

"It would seem so. Apparently, her male traveling companion had told Caruthers he accompanied our niece since women shouldn't travel Surrey roads alone. He gave some tale of highwaymen in the area, but if the comments of the cook and maids are to believed, said gentleman is quite dashing."

"Is that right?" Ah, clever man. She'd heard about highwaymen, but she suspected the man's intent was to ingratiate himself into her good graces. Sly boots, but it wouldn't work. "I do hope Amanda's penchant for immaturity has worn off since we last saw her."

"Well, hope does spring eternal, but in all practicality, I rather doubt Amanda has changed. She is Gregory's offspring, after all."

She rolled her eyes at her brother's droll tone. "If not, we have a problem. A petulant child paired with a dashing male on the prowl could be a disaster." Maggie shook her head as cold dread seeped in to steal the joy and excitement of the afternoon. A handsome man could do more damage to a young girl's equilibrium than anything else. "Well, I shall simply set her straight. An untried girl of eighteen doesn't know her own mind, let alone have any control over her own romantic notions. More likely she's in love with the idea of being in love. Silly chit. There's more to love and marriage than dreaming."

"Indeed." Alfred snickered into his hand. "No matter, tea should be quite entertaining. Perhaps your grand affair will begin today."

"Don't be a nodcock." Maggie rolled her eyes, her smile back in place. "I'm not in the mood for a scandal this afternoon."

Nor did she know if she ever would be. After all, creating a scandal needed weeks of planning. At the present time, all she wanted to do was sort out Amanda's mess.

Chapter Two

Stephen Oliver Tarkington paced the length of the parlor. With each step, his annoyance grew and expanded until his fingers curled into fists so tight that his fingertips dug into his palms. He clasped his hands behind his back to hide the worst of his ire. Clenching his teeth, he studied the pink-and-gold striped wallpaper, decorated with impossibly tiny vines and roses. The theme carried over throughout the rest of the room. From the gilt-painted legs of the delicate furniture to the plush, pink velvet cushions on every available sitting surface, to the Oriental rugs done in mauves, golds and greens, the room screamed a feminine viewpoint, and one that was very finicky. It spoke of a mind that would be hard-pressed to change, of a will as iron and as tough as old torture devices in the Tower of London.

It was enough to make him decidedly ill. A grin curved his lips. He'd never turned down a challenge, and the prospect of meeting the elderly owner of this house set his pulse to racing. He'd always had great luck charming ladies of any age; one dowager holder of the purse strings should be no exception.

"Mr. Tarkington, do return to the settee. I'm feeling rather lonely here by myself." The whine from his traveling companion set his nerves on edge.

Good heavens, does she need to complain about everything? He swung around so fast the tails on his blue superfine jacket flared. He darted a glance to a straight-backed chair across from the young woman, but the chit's ancient nanny dozed, oblivious to her surroundings. Soft snores issued from her slack mouth. "Miss Manning, remind me again why you must seek an audience with your aunt? Why is it necessary to be here in person? Could you not accomplish your task with correspondence?" And thus give him further opportunity to enchant her and stake his claim.

The pretty, young blonde peered at him from beneath the brim of her poke bonnet trimmed with sky-blue ribbons to match her gown. "Why not?"

"What do you mean?"

He'd met her three weeks ago in London, ran directly into her as she darted about one of the clichéd tourist sites as he was merely passing through. After making his apologies, her blue eyes and heart-shaped face had attracted his interest, and once he'd ascertained, thanks to her endless stream of mostly nonsensical babble about fashions and people-watching, that she was a veritable heiress, he'd applied enough charm to hook her infatuation. He'd asked after her direction, and upon finding her staying in London with an acquaintance and her elderly companion, he secured permission to call, spending most of his free time paying court to her, much to the humor of his contemporaries.

They wouldn't be laughing once he found someone with enough wealth to become a benefactor in his bid for Parliament.

"As I told you in the coach, Aunt Margaret is sponsoring me during the Season. Besides that, she controls any money I might spend—on a wardrobe or otherwise—and if you and I will be married, she must give us her blessing. I am her only heir, you see." Her tone conveyed him bacon-brained as only the young could do.

Stephen's eyes widened. He cleared his throat. "I beg your pardon, but did you say married?" As of yet, he hadn't asked for her hand, hadn't danced with her, let alone shared a kiss—chaste or otherwise.

Her nod set the pheasant feather on her hat bobbing. "Of course! Is that not the point of this trip?" Her eyes twinkled. "A man whose only intent is a flirtation would not willingly wish an introduction to a lady's relative if he had no interest in the future."

"Indeed."

She bounced on the settee. "I had no idea I'd have such luck my first week in town!"

"Imagine that." At the last second, he stifled a groan. Botheration. What now? He'd meant to string her along a bit longer before making any decision. If the miss had her way, he'd be trussed and reciting vows before the week was out.

Stephen resumed pacing, but his thoughts were far from impending nuptials or finding himself snared in the parson's mousetrap. He'd been leg-shackled twice before. He wasn't looking to have his heart crushed or his life disrupted a third time. To his way of thinking, keeping a mistress was the best of all options. Conducting a relationship based on compatibility between the sheets seemed to be what he excelled at, and when making up for shortcomings with a bauble or two didn't work, he sent the bit of muslin packing.

No one got hurt, and best of all, his heart wasn't engaged. Trying to anticipate what a female needed to keep her happy seemed beyond his ken.

He swung around to ask Amanda another question, but he caught her mid-stream in what appeared to be a rather wordy one-sided conversation. He'd had no idea she'd been talking.

"I wonder what one should wear to parties and routs when one knows she will be imminently engaged." Her eyes gleamed with castles in the clouds only she could see. "Oh, and where should we announce our engagement? Do you think Aunt Margaret will throw a huge ball? We want the most attention we can summon. The more people who know, the better chance at presents."

Oh, bother.

"Miss Manning, has it occurred to you that neither of us is in love? I'd like to think you hold me in some esteem before I offer for your hand—if that eventuality even occurs." The bitterness of his situation soured his stomach. If he wanted to do right by his country in Parliament and bring issues to light that would help the classes meet, he needed befriend someone with influence. It would seem accessing Miss Manning's aunt through her would not meet that need. Damn it all to hell.

"Of course you are not in love with me. Men seldom fall quickly."

"Is that so?" As if she had mountains of experience. He narrowed his eyes. "Pray continue." *I must be out of my mind to consider aligning myself with a female so young and untried.*

"Well, the moment I met you, I knew my life would be forever changed. The way you kept me from falling when we collided and the considerate way you asked after my health both point to a future between us. Add to that your height, your manly build and roiling gray eyes and it will be easy to reach that state of affairs." She nodded as if he were but a mere laundry list of physical traits.

Roiling eyes? I think I might retch on my boots. "Ah, so you're infatuated with me?"

A smile curved her lips. "Perhaps, and it would be much easier if you'd be more sympathetic to the thought of a union between us."

Stephen counted to ten in order to summon patience. "How can I be when we've only just met? I'd like to know a bit more about you as a person before a run at the marriage altar."

As quickly as it came, the smile vanished in the face of a fierce pout. "You are no fun, Mr. Tarkington."

"So I've been told by more females than you." Stephen crossed the room and alighted next to her on the settee, across from the snoring Nanny Beatrice. "Tell me about your aunt. I'd rather be informed before bearding the dragon."

"There's not much to say. She's old, and I've heard folks refer to her as eccentric, some even say scandalous, but they must be wrong. Aunt Margaret doesn't have a scandalous bone in her body. She doesn't *do* anything. Why else would she have chosen to hide away in Surrey of all places?" Amanda shrugged. "I have spent a few summers here with her. She's not much fun. Since Uncle Robert died, she's changed, always puttering outside for hours on end, doing God only knows what."

He covered his amusement with a frown. To the young, older people finding interesting pursuits was inconceivable. "Does she often get up to town?" The idea of being consigned to the country with nothing to entertain him sent a cold chill down his spine. How did the woman spend her time besides gardening?

"I think she might visit twice a year to buy gowns or visit with friends, and she has to go for my Season this year." A smug smile accompanied the statement. "I do hope she won't make a nuisance of herself. She needs to stay with the overzealous mamas and other companions. I shall be quite busy dancing and furthering the acquaintance of the *ton's* finest."

"You cut me to the quick, Miss Manning. I had thought you had your sights set on taking my name." He laid a hand over his heart in a bout of theatrics, never mind the flash of relief in his chest.

"Oh, pish-posh, Mr. Tarkington. How you do go on. You said yourself a union between us is only a possibility." She giggled then took up a fashion magazine from a nearby tabletop. "I'm told all the best English marriages are in name only."

"Some are." His stomach clenched. "Is that what you think would be between us? Name only so you're free to cuckold me whenever it pleases you?"

"Well, yes. It is a big world after all, and unlikely I'll marry for love."

His frown deepened. Her view of the world, so jaded for one so young, stuck in his throat. "Ah." Right now, it felt more and more like a very small pond indeed. Foreboding climbed his spine. Perhaps doing the pretty with Miss Amanda

Manning was not in his best interest after all. Yet for the moment, she was the best chance of access to a money and someone with a sponsorship ability he'd found. "Forgive me if I injure your American sensibilities, but your information is not exactly correct. Many English matches have been made for love."

Stephen held his own parents as an example of the grandiose ideal a marriage could be. They'd been together for thirty-six years, one year longer than he was old, and from all accounts, they were as much in love with each other as they had been on their wedding day. That's what he constantly searched for in a union. That's what he consistently hadn't found. There had to be something over and above that first mind-muddling sexual tension, a friendship of sorts, a challenge to maintain interest in a relationship. So far, everything beyond the carnal eluded him.

There *was* a certain base joy in burying his member in a woman's warm center or of licking a path between her velvet soft breasts. Seeing a woman's pleasure, hearing it in the little sounds she made while in the throes of passion, was his reward.

Amanda's trilling laughter cut into his thoughts and effectively killed the cloud of lusty remembrances. "I plan to lead you a merry chase before I allow you to catch me, Mr. Tarkington. Don't think I don't know you're after my aunt's money."

The thought of being leg-shackled to such a young lady turned his stomach. Courting young misses wasn't the option he wanted to spend time doing at the moment. He wanted to serve his country and make it a better place for everyone, so that the next generation wouldn't need to struggle.

He stifled a sigh. Perhaps he'd been without the comforts of a woman for too long, which would be the only reason he'd entertained this hair-brained scheme to begin with. What he needed was a mistress, to embark on an affair. He glanced at Amanda. An *older* woman, he silently amended. Yet at the moment, that was highly unlikely to happen.

Bugger.

She tucked a strand of hair beneath her bonnet. "I want a bit of fun before we decide anything, and as my father always says, 'a bird in hand is better than two in the bush'. I may be young, but I do have a brain in my head."

God, spare me from this proverb-quoting American. "My, how fickle the young are. You bounce from one extreme to the other, my dear. The dragons at Almack's or any of the other fortresses of female virtue frown on a young lady deporting herself in an impure manner."

"I am not doing any such thing. I am merely preparing for every eventuality. If you do not come up to scratch, I shall set my cap for another man. You won't be my only option, I'm sure." She looked at him, a vague smile gracing her lips before she resumed her perusal of the magazine.

Dear Lord, how many bucks much younger than he would she lead about from the nose before she made a choice? Was she acting scatterbrained due to youth, fickleness or did all American chits think like her? In the end, did it matter?

He quelled the urge to run out of house, run off the property and keep running until he hit the main road and could curry favor with a coach or wagon headed for parts unknown. Getting into Parliament wasn't as important as his sanity. He'd find another way to reach his objective.

Of course Amanda wouldn't understand his annoyance. To her, life laid spread out in sparkling wonderment full of people to meet and things to conquer. For him, he'd already lived what seemed like two lifetimes—and failed at both attempts. He didn't want the rest of his life to become an eternity. Stephen shoved the aged feeling from his mind. A glance around the parlor didn't reveal the spirits he desperately desired. If he wasn't so set on obtaining his goals—

The door opened and the butler entered, pushing a silver tea service on a polished, wheeled wooden cart. "I apologize for the interruption. Lady Parker wished me to offer you tea as you wait. She will be down momentarily."

Amanda jumped to her feet and clapped her gloved hands. "Splendid! I'm famished. Aunt Margaret always serves the best tea."

The sleeping companion didn't stir. The irony of the situation didn't escape him. If he'd ever wanted to ravage Miss Manning, he should have done it before tea arrived. His gaze slid back to her as she raided the tea service. Crumbs decorated her modest bosom while she shoved cakes into her mouth as if they would suddenly vanish. A small shiver shook him. She wasn't exactly the epitome of femininity, not even in a fresh, untouched virginal sort of way. He'd been daft to consider an alliance. From this point forward, debutantes and, most especially, Incomparables were off limits. He simply didn't have the patience for their antics and wild mood swings.

Now counting the minutes until he could polity escape the tedium, he said, "Will the wait to see Lady Parker be much longer?" Stephen rose to stroll the room at a sedate pace. He pinned the butler a glance.

One of the stately man's gray-tipped eyebrows rose. "Lady Parker keeps her own schedule, and you did arrive a day early." He bowed slightly from the waist then exited the room.

"This is outside of enough." Stephen bit off a curse as he accepted a teacup from Amanda. "Just because a person is advanced in years does not entitle them to adhere to bad manners." He took a deep swig of the tea, swallowing it down then proceeded to cough as the hot liquid hit the back of his throat. "Damnation!" He rushed to the tea tray to hunt for a napkin. When would the old woman make an appearance?

"Now, now, I do not tolerate blatant cursing in this house unless you have a very good reason." A vibrant, female voice intruded into the room. "Lack of patience is not one of them."

"I apologize." He dabbed at his lips with a linen napkin, not at all pleased to meet yet another female for whom he had no use. Slowly, Stephen turned and faced the woman who belonged to the voice.

In a gesture much like the one Amanda had made earlier, the new arrival tucked a strand of dark brown hair into her coif, which framed her round face and set off her roses-and-cream complexion. Her blue eyes sparkled like lake water on a sunny day. "I am Lady Margaret Parker. Pleased to meet you Mr...?" Her voice trailed off as she held out her right hand, her expression clearly expectant.

The little tea he'd swallowed threatened to make a return trip. Not only was Miss Manning's aunt not elderly or old, she was still young and most decidedly alert. His chest smarted as if he'd taken a blow. She was no dragon, to be sure, and she was easily one of the most desirable women he'd clapped eyes upon. All his previously crafted plans to win over an old woman dissolved into ether. With as much dignity as he could, he set the teacup on a low table then rushed over the floor. He scooped up the proffered hand, bringing it to his lips and pressed a brief kiss on her knuckle. The pleasant sent of lilacs rose from her skin and lingered in his nose after he released her hand.

"I am Mr. Stephen Tarkington. Please, call me Stephen."

Her rosy lips curved in a grin. "Thank you, but I will reserve judgment on whether I'll use your first name."

Stephen blinked, thoroughly chastised. Perhaps she'd be a tougher challenge than the old woman he'd thought he'd easily charm. "Please accept my apologies for my assumption."

She nodded. "However, you may call me Margaret, or later, if I deem you trustworthy, Maggie." She swept past him and alighted on the settee next to Amanda. "How do you and my niece know each other?" Margaret busied herself with the tea service, pouring out a cup then adding one sugar cube.

Why couldn't he speak? Surprise gripped him, yet lingering on the edges was shock that he wasn't the bat he'd expected. Instead, she could easily be the type of woman he'd enjoy chasing. When the silence stretched out between them, she cleared her throat, lifting her gaze to his.

"I, uh, when I came across Miss Manning and her nanny in London, I didn't trust that a young miss and her ancient handler could see the main sights of London on their own, so I volunteered my services. In due course, I heard about their upcoming trip and thought it my duty to accompany them to Surrey in the advent of an attack from highwaymen."

"I see, and I'm sure that by doing this great and courageous deed, you thought to attract my niece's attention to your bachelor state, or," she arched an eyebrow, "gain my everlasting regard that you held Amanda's safety dear and I might reciprocate by loosening my purse strings?"

Sweat trickled down Stephen's spine. This was not how the afternoon was supposed to go.

"Do come and sit down, Mr. Tarkington. I dislike carrying on a conversation when my guests are flung out across the room."

Stephen stumbled across the floor and dropped into the nearest chair before his knees gave out. Lady Parker moved a teaspoon through the amber liquid in her glass, around and around, her pale, slim fingers grasping the silver with such grace. "The idea was recently tossed around."

"Then you are interested in wedding her?"

"I'm not sure." What a bramble. "Perhaps I'm desirous of more information." He wasn't enamored of a betrothal to the niece when furthering the acquaintance with the delectable aunt had now presented itself.

"Oh, bother, Mr. Tarkington, it's not a question for the ages. You're here. She's here, and looking at you with calf's eyes. Do you desire an engagement or don't you?"

He forgot his manners and openly gawked at Lady Parker. Her blunt speaking would reduce him to ribbons in a trice, yet also fascinated him. Who was this mysterious creature? "Perhaps if Miss Manning grows into looks and temperament like her aunt." He tacked on the last to charm himself into the aunt's good graces.

"That remains to be seen." Yet a smile flirted with her lips.

She was not what he expected and now he couldn't comprehend the idea that Amanda's aunt was very much his own age, and beautiful. The wine-colored gown she wore hugged her full breasts while the toe of her black velvet slippers peeked out. What would her ankle look like above that slipper? Did she possess high arches? Would his caress tickle her foot or was she more sensitive higher up on the leg, perhaps the back of her knee or her inner thigh?

The discreet tinkle of her teaspoon against the cup's rim yanked him from his thoughts. Mere seconds had passed while he'd mused, but to him it had felt like days. He blinked, wishing his head would clear. "All future plans are dependent on your good humor and blessing." *However, plans are subject to change...*

Margaret huffed and sipped her tea, her calculating gaze resting on him as if she tried to see into his soul.

"Auntie, Mr. Tarkington is ever so pleasant." Amanda touched her aunt's arm and simpered when she gained Margaret's attention. "He's escorted me about London, taking me to numerous tourist sites. He was quite solicitous while in my company; even engaging Nanny Beatrice in conversation—when she was awake." Her tittering laughter set Stephen's teeth on edge. "We rode a carriage in Rotten Row then had a flavored ice and watched the people once. I think you'll like him."

"Mmhmm." Lady Parker set her teacup down. "Child, I know you are excited about entering the adult world of courtship, dinners and dancing, but there are other things to consider. Is it possible you only think you fancy Mr. Tarkington because he's the first suitor to pay attention to you?"

"A suitor? I beg your pardon, Lady Parker, that is not exactly true—" Stephen immediately broke off at the sharp look she shot him.

"I will deal with you in a moment." Her eyes flashed a warning before she regarded her niece again. "Do you know what Mr. Tarkington does for a living?"

"No, but—"

"Do you know who his family is, how connected he is, or his history?"

"Not yet." A note of sullenness crept into Amanda's voice. "What does it matter, Aunt? You cannot tell me who to love or even to marry. If I want Mr. Tarkington, I will get him."

"That also remains to be seen." One corner of Margaret's mouth tipped upward. Stephen didn't trust that half-grin. "Has he told you anything personal about himself or has he spent all his time with you, paying you compliments and filling your head full of empty promises you have no idea if he'll keep? Will he be willing to uproot his life to America if you decide that is where you want to live?"

Oh, God, resettle in America? Stephen choked again on his tea. Leaving England would be counterproductive to his plans.

"Aunt Margaret!" Horror propelled the exclamation from Amanda's rosebud mouth. "Must everything be decided in one afternoon?"

"You seemed willing enough to have it so an hour ago when you arrived and told Caruthers of your intentions."

"Why do you have to be so difficult?"

Lady Parker's grin bloomed. "Because I am quite accomplished at it."

"Maybe I shall change my mind in the face of all this fuss. You're quite determined to oppose my match with him." Amanda crossed her arms over her chest and pouted. "You see, Mr. Tarkington, she is no fun at all."

As much as he wanted to protest the inquisition, Stephen quelled the urge to say anything. He'd encountered women of Lady Parker's stamp before and knew they'd be stubborn if provoked. He also knew they required special handling. For the moment, he contented himself with studying her, as if sizing up an opponent. "Perhaps that depends on your interpretation of amusement."

Amanda's lips thinned. "I am certain we will get around to discussing such things, Aunt Margaret."

"Ah, then you've once more changed your mind and swung back to deciding he should court you. We shall see." For long moments, tension-filled silence sat heavy in the room so thick the ticking of the carriage clock on a bookshelf clamored in the void. Lady Parker took her teacup in hand and sipped. While staring out a window, a frown formed on her kissable mouth. "I will allow you and Mr. Tarkington to be in each other's company while you are here on my property. Of course, I will always be in your presence so I can monitor the courtship—if this visit comes to that. After spending time here with me, if you two appear to be able to make a go of it, I'll give you my blessing and send you on your way."

"And if not?" Stephen leaned forward in the high-backed chair. The way she held herself and the tilt of her chin spoke of a confidence he'd not seen in a female for a long time. It intrigued him.

Margaret deposited her teacup on its saucer. "Then, I will send you back to London and begin Amanda's Season here in Surrey as I'd planned to do all along. Once I'm sure she's capable enough to withstand the rigors and pitfalls of Society, I shall accompany her to London. After that, her future is in fate's hands. You are not the only fish in the sea, Mr. Tarkington. I want the best for my niece."

Her superior attitude rubbed at him, even if he agreed with her censure of his farcical relationship with the chit. Why did she not consider him worthy enough for her niece? "Perhaps that is not for you to say, Lady Parker."

She leveled the full weight of her gaze on him. Stephen swore he felt it as if she'd slapped him. "It is if either of you want to see one pence of my money. Controlling a fortune is not a fulfilling endeavor if you have no one of meaning to share it with." Margaret rose and shook out the wrinkles from her gown. "Amanda, your old room has been readied for you. Why don't you have yourself a lie down? I'll be up soon to make plans for the dressmaker. She'll arrive tomorrow for fittings and pinnings."

Amanda clapped her hands together then clasped them beneath her chin. "That would be lovely, Auntie."

He narrowed his eyes as Amanda quit the room. *How easily her attention swings.*

Lady Parker continued, "Mr. Tarkington, a word if you please."

Stephen nodded but the haughty woman swept by him and went through the doorway before he'd gained his feet. This one represented the very challenge he pined for. Any woman with spirit like hers had to possess passion behind closed doors. What would it take to release that passion?

A grin curled his lips as he followed in her lilac-scented wake. How he'd enjoy furthering his acquaintance with Lady Parker. He whistled a jaunty tune.

The day is looking better already.

Chapter Three

As Maggie passed a maid in the hallway, she laid a hand on the young woman's arm. "Jeanette, be a dear and pop into the back parlor. Nanny Beatrice has fallen asleep. Could you please wake her and settle her into a guest room?"

"Right away, ma'am."

"Oh, and offer Miss Manning a cup of chocolate. It'll go a long way into improving her mood."

"Yes, my lady." The girl curtsied and retreated along the hall.

"It could also be considered a bribe." A smooth chuckle behind her sent heat into Maggie's cheeks.

She hated that she reacted to him as if she were a schoolroom miss. "It is. How shrewd of you to notice." She wiped her sweaty palms on the skirt of her dress. "Now then, Mr. Tarkington, I fancy a walk through the grounds as I feel outdoor exercise clears the mind and improves the spirit better than stifling rooms."

"Whatever you think is best, Lady Parker. I am here on your good grace."

His smooth baritone voice sent shivers over her skin. "Indeed, you are, especially as you're uninvited, I might remind you." Maggie grinned at his effrontery. He was quite the sly boots, but if he had designs on her niece, she'd disabuse him of the notion quickly. She couldn't put her finger on why, other than he had too much town bronze for an eighteen-year-old girl. "I might also remind you that my outriders are more than adequate to see to my niece's protection in the future."

She led him down the hallway and then out a side door that opened into a garden. Alfred knelt in the dirt, pulling weeds from the primrose border. "Alfie, this is Mr. Tarkington." She gestured a hand toward her companion. "He's come to visit along with Amanda, in what capacity remains to be seen, although I suspect it was simply to deliver her to me from the kindness of his heart."

"Ah." Alfred's concentration remained on his plants.

"He and I are going for a short stroll. Perhaps to the rose arbor."

"Oh?" Her brother looked between her and Stephen, the afternoon sun glinting off his spectacle lenses. He took a handkerchief from a pocket and wiped his hands. "I'll accompany you. Wouldn't want to attract another scandal, eh Mags?"

Blasted Alfie. What is he about? She glowered at him, but he merely grinned as he stood. "Why not? I'm always looking for a good one."

"Indeed you are." He held out a hand to Stephen. "I'm Alfred Manning, Maggie's younger brother. I'm visiting with her until the Season concludes after which I'll escort Amanda back to America." He readjusted his spectacles. "I will allow you the stroll if you mind your manners. Mags has a penchant for trouble, so be alert."

"Troublesome females are the best kind." Stephen shook Alfred's hand, a rogue's grin on his face. A dimple winked in his chin, offset by a strong jaw and Roman nose, while the sun caught his eyes and turned the gray to silver. "Please, call me Stephen." He slid his bright gaze to her and gave her a blatant wink. "Your sister has quite recalcitrantly refused my request to do the same."

Heat continued to burn Maggie's cheeks. She raised a hand thinking to fiddle with the brim of her bonnet then remembered she hadn't worn one out. *Damn and blast.* She dropped her hand to her side. "I said I needed to trust him first before the intimacy of a first name was used." The more she tried not to stare at the sensuous curve of his lips, the more she *did* stare. What would they feel like against hers? What sort of a kisser was Mr. Tarkington? Dear Lord, of all the men to fantasize about, why did it have to be *him*? She shook her head and transferred her gaze to her brother, hoping to change the subject.

"No time like the present to strike up a cozy friendship." Stephen, apparently, wouldn't be side-tracked. He turned toward her, his grin widening. "It would please me to no end if you would call me Stephen..." He cocked an eyebrow. "...Margaret."

A shiver careened down her spine as he pronounced her name with such care. She imagined it on a whisper in the dark as he lay on the pillow next to hers. Her tongue was glued to the roof of her mouth, and she gaped as if she were barely out of the schoolroom. She knew nothing about this man except his name, but his proximity to her and the smoky tones of his voice sent waves of need crashing through her insides.

Her brother narrowed his eyes with a smirk. "You know, it seems Stephen is quite *grand*, eh, Mags? Wouldn't you like to know more about his affairs?" Alfred barely managed to turn his chuckle into a choking cough. "You know, to protect our niece's interests."

"I'm not certain at this point." She hated that Stephen attempted to manipulate the situation to his advantage, hated that her brother tried to goad her into going forward with her plan. "Botheration." Maggie huffed and blew a wisp of hair from her face and focused on *him*. "It will remain Mr. Tarkington for now." The man deserved a severe dressing-down. "Shall we proceed on our walk?" First and foremost, she wanted to know his intentions toward her niece. "We have much to discuss."

"Absolutely." Stephen offered his arm. "I am anxious to hear more about what I suspect is a colorful past on your part."

"Then prepare to be vastly disappointed. If you haven't gotten wind of rumors, there aren't any stories to share." As she slid her hand through his crooked arm, Alfred snickered into his sleeve. *Traitorous brother.* The heat of Stephen's sun-warmed sleeve seeped into her fingertips, and beneath her palm, his bicep flexed. A nice, solid arm, one that would keep her firmly anchored against his chest if he were to sweep her into an embrace, and he smelled clean like soap and citrus. Flutters tickled her belly.

"Ah, a lady of mystery. Will it be a challenge to coax out the tales I wonder?"

"That largely depends on why you are here, Mr. Tarkington."

"Stephen."

Maggie huffed again. The man wouldn't be dissuaded. "Stephen." She drew him down the path. "Perhaps you should tell me what your intentions are toward my niece."

"Straight to the point, eh? I rather like that about you. You waste no time in idle conversation." He patted her hand. Awareness jolted up Maggie's arm, but she let his familiarity go. It was... nice to be in a male's proximity again. "Amanda is... young."

"Yes, and in her last letter, she had but one thought in her head—to enjoy her Season with as many admirers as possible. Imagine my surprise when dear Amanda shows up at my home a day early and in a stranger's company."

"It wasn't to be helped. I'm afraid I took advantage of the opportunity."

"I'm sure you did, and I hope that is all you took advantage of. You look to be very resourceful." Unscrupulous men turned her stomach, nor could she abide wanting her niece's leavings.

"No need to fear on that count. Deflowering virgins isn't on my agenda."

"Which begs the question, what is your agenda? I find it highly suspect you've come here to Surrey only as a safe escort."

"As if I had a reason to lie."

She cocked her head, considering her next words. "Amanda does not need the attentions of a man nearly twice her age." Maggie quickened her pace, anxious to reach the rose arbor where they could talk without fear of being overheard. Though she didn't care a whit for her already tarnished reputation, she didn't want Amanda's sullied by a private conversation.

"How astute of you, but one year off." The corner of his mouth nearest her quirked upward. "I'm five and thirty."

"Ah." Her pulse increased. He was only three years older than she, and very much of an age for *her* attentions. "So, tell me why you've chosen a girl barely out of the schoolroom for your romantic interests." Her low heels scraped against the flagstones as they entered the half-moon-shaped rose arbor.

"Romantic interests?" Stephen released her hand and walked ahead of her, the dappled sunlight through the rose leaves playing shadows over his face. "I have an interest in your niece, but it has nothing to do with romance."

"Not according to her, so tell me, what do your interests have to do with?" She followed him along the path beneath the lattices, her gaze caressing his broad shoulders and the fit of his legs in his cream-colored trousers. What did he do for a living that kept him in such fine form? "Now would be a good time to state your case or plead your cause."

He clasped his hands behind his back. "Do you want the truth?"

"Preferably."

Slowly, he swung around and stared boldly at her. "Or would you rather I spin you a tale?" One eyebrow rose in question.

"Oh, I'm certain you've regaled any number of women with stories. I'm surprised you're still single. That is," she narrowed her eyes, "you are unattached, are you not?" She had to know for Amanda's sake.

"I am, but in the interest of full disclosure, I will tell you that I have been married twice before. Both ended horribly." A flicker of dark emotion clouded his eyes, but when he shook his head, the shadows faded.

"I see, yet you intend to wed my niece."

"No. She is the one talking of matrimony. I'm not sure the wedded state agrees with me." He waved off her concern as if the subject matter were of no consequence.

"Ah." What an enigma he was. She bit her bottom lip and willed her knees to stop wobbling. His cocky attitude and inherent confidence played havoc with her insides. "My niece's well-being is more important than how entertaining you promise to be." And he had the air of a man who would be *very* entertaining. Her breath hitched.

"Fair enough." The gentle breeze played with his hair, ruffling it into raven waves. "I am in need of someone with money who might sponsor my bid for Parliament."

"And you've chosen me, and thereby using Amanda as an entry?" She didn't appreciate being hunted for money alone.

"As terrible as it sounds, yes."

Her stomach pitched. "You sound extremely mercenary."

"Unfortunately, life requires one to be that way at times."

"It does, but I am afraid I cannot sponsor someone of your seemingly loose morals, Stephen." She enjoyed how his name felt on her lips, but would refrain from uttering it again.

"You wanted the truth. I gave it to you."

Maggie paused near a trellis covered with climbing miniature pink roses. "As I told you before, you or she won't see any of my money unless I have good reason to part with it. At this point I see no good reason, especially now in light of your plan. Perhaps you should explain your political ideals further." She shoved away her disappointment. If he was nothing more than a fortune hunter looking to line his pockets at her expense and that of the British people, so be it. She'd have him escorted from her property faster than he could draw his next breath.

Yet she hoped he'd prove her wrong. A glimmer of an idea took hold in her mind. Though he was vastly inappropriate for Amanda, he could be just the type of man she needed for an affair. Should she follow through on the thought?

"I grew up on the London streets. My family was destitute. My parents had more children than money or common sense. Everyone I knew was poor also." He paced before a line of dark-leafed white rose bushes. "For many years I dreamed of being someone important while the reality of that becoming true kept staring me in the face. There was more than enough evidence against me that dictated I should have become a chimney sweep, a lowly accountant, or if I was lucky, a banker."

"I can imagine how those circumstances would either give a man motivation or desperation." She threaded her fingers together at her waist. "I was fortunate enough that my family didn't want for anything, but we were far from rich."

"What does your father do?"

"He's a career Navy man. Set to be an admiral soon. My oldest brother is an attorney while Alfie is a botanist. I admire a man with aspirations and the know-how to accomplish them."

"It makes a difference when the parents are happy despite their circumstances. The only thing my father lacked was a good job and money in his pocket to support the family, but he was a dreamer. Mum didn't seem to mind."

Maggie sat on a wooden bench near one of the trellises. "And that is why you want the money, for security, to make a better life for yourself than your father had?" She glanced at him, but no matter how hard she tried, she couldn't see him as desperate.

"No. I have enough money to live quite comfortably on for the next several years." He leaned forward and plucked one of the creamy blooms from the bush. "I worked hard and beat the odds, Margaret. I went to school. I even found a benefactor, who put me through university." He twirled the rose between his thumb and forefinger, unmindful of the thorns. "Without that man's help, I would have been a nothing, like everyone else on my childhood street, fighting, struggling to survive in a world that is rigidly divided by class, wealth and sheer dumb luck."

"Believe me, I do understand that." Since she was a transplant to England, she couldn't help but notice the extreme class divisions. "Why could not this benefactor sponsor your bid into Parliament? He obviously has enough money."

"This was my plan, but the man's heart failed him six months ago and put an end to the notion. As luck, or perhaps life, would have it, his son inherited the funds."

"Ah, and the son wasn't interested in backing a man whom he didn't know."

"Yes, you understand the gist of it."

"I'm truly sorry for your difficulties."

"Thank you. I make do." Stephen appeared not to have heard her. "I am a successful import man with close ties to the Americas, France and Spain. I am able to procure a wide array of goods and sell them at adequate prices here. It keeps me busy and comfortable." He pulled a few petals from the rose and let the breeze carry them off his palm. "Regardless, I'm compelled to give the upcoming generation an unbiased opportunity. We need to dedicate ourselves to bettering relations with other countries and cultivate their aid if we what to propel ourselves into the future. England is not the be all and end all."

"This is true. I've heard my father comment on that fact more than once."

"I'd like to introduce laws or enact laws that would lessen the gap between the wealthy and the poor, or provide more opportunities for the less fortunate, and put a greater emphasis on education and industry." Passion laced his statement, while he crushed the rose in his fist. "I want to take a place in Parliament, but without a sponsor or someone with high-born connections, my hands are proverbially tied. The Lords will continue to bicker their lives away at the expense of the common man."

"You have summed the situation up nicely." How encouraging to find a gentleman who touted the same ideals she believed in. "I wish you luck in the endeavor." Thrills spiraled up her spine as she imagined hours of heated debate and conversation they could have together.

He nodded, but kept his gaze on the rose. Another few petals fell to the path. "In the event I am unable to secure a backer, I can try to use a fortune to buy my way in. After all," a blast of bitter laugh escaped him, "there are enough corrupt men in Parliament that a big enough purse will surely catch an eye or two. Doesn't matter how I get there as long as I can make a difference with my life."

Maggie mulled over his words. He didn't appear to be a stupid man, in it only for the fame and notoriety a Parliament seat would provide. "From another man's mouth, your story would smack of make believe, yet from you, I feel you tell the truth."

"How so? You didn't appear to believe anything else I've said."

A sigh eased between her lips. "Where Amanda is concerned, I'm very protective, but hearing you speak your case and seeing the passion in your eyes, I believe you are sincere. It gives me hope for this country." She clasped her hands in her lap as he chucked the destroyed rose into a bush.

"Thank you. Coming from you, that is high praise indeed." His smile made her skin burn hotter than sitting in the sun.

"It's too bad you won't offer your suit to Amanda. I would have liked to help you on your quest." She'd finally heard a cause she could throw her support behind, and she certainly had enough money. "Parliament could benefit with a level head as well as a man with an actual plan for change over tradition."

Unless... She shifted on the bench. Would he be willing to go along with her idea?

"Yes, well, I think perhaps it was ill-advised of me to single Amanda out." A calculating light entered his eyes and he walked toward her. "What about you, Margaret?"

"We were not talking about me." That expression of mischief on his face sent a wave of need coursing through her body.

"I think we should." The corners of his lips tipped in a smile. "Amanda told me your husband died some time ago. Perhaps you'd be willing to put yourself on the market? I would imagine you'd catch more eyes than an untried girl just out of school."

"Don't be silly." She laughed, thoroughly amused, and alternately on edge, by his antics. "I'm well past marriageable age, even if I wanted another husband."

"Then you are not looking for another match?" Stephen moved behind the bench and paused with a hand resting near her shoulder.

"I didn't say that." She thought back over her union to Robert and stifled a giggle. Over the course of time, she'd learned to love him, even had a child with him, but had it been an all-consuming passion that made her forget everything else? No. It had been a staid, even-keeled romance that hadn't challenged her.

"But you did not agree either." His chuckle sent shivers over her skin, chilling her even though the sun bore down. "Women like you deserve a man's regard or, at the very least, the thrill of being chased."

Maggie tamped a shiver. "Perhaps, the next time, it won't be me who is pursued. Perhaps I'll do the chasing."

"Are you offering?"

Was she? Though she'd talked flippantly with Alfie about having one grand affair that would set tongues wagging, her stomach trembled. Did Stephen Tarkington fit the bill? "I might, if you promise to leave Amanda alone."

"Ah, a better deal, eh?" His rich chuckle loosed more tingles down her spine. "Is it adventure you crave, Maggie?" He drew a finger down one side of her neck, glided it along her skin where her shoulder met and rested his hand there, his fingers lightly trailing over her collarbone.

She closed her eyes. Gooseflesh lingered everywhere he'd plied his fingers. Tingles danced down her spine. Warmth seeped between her thighs. It had been a long time since she'd had a man's interest. "I wouldn't mind a bit of spice."

"Spice is fine, or is it the scandal you want?" Stephen rubbed a fingertip along her collarbone and then traced the lace edge of her bodice, his touch the veriest of whispers over the top of one breast.

Would he dare to go lower and caress her aching flesh? "Scandal has come to mind once or twice." Her head lolled on the opposite shoulder from where he played. She kept her eyes closed in order to fully enjoy the situation, one moment more before she censured him. "I thought that if I found myself in a big enough tangle I'd attract the attention of a like-minded gentleman." Why was she telling him this, when he was but a stranger?

"For what purpose? A fling, an affair, or are you searching for more?" His finger, hot against her skin, dipped beneath her bodice and her shift.

Maggie whimpered. The weak heat of the spring sun couldn't compete with the flames Stephen had awakened inside her. Being here in the garden, with his hand on her, was highly inappropriate. They could both be in terrible trouble if caught. Her lips curved with a grin. But then, she did just admit she'd like the scandal. "I want a grand affair, something that will burn so bright the English gossips will talk about it for years."

"Why, sweet Maggie? Are you lonely?"

"I'm not sure." Her breath caught. It took all her willpower to remain still beneath his touch, but oh, how she wished he'd give her more relief.

"Too bad." His finger slid lower and brushed her nipple. Back and forth he teased the puckered tip, pebbling it into a frenzy of need.

Maggie couldn't help the moan that escaped her.

"Have you missed this, the exquisite torture only a man can bring? I hear your sounds of enjoyment. What do you want most, Lady Parker?" His breath warmed the shell of her ear as he withdrew his hand from her bodice and put an end to the brief, wonderful torture.

Her moan turned into a whine of protest.

"Perhaps I can give it to you." His smug chuckle slid over her skin like silk.

She snapped open her eyes. Longing gripped her. Yes, why not? If any man was right for a scandal, Stephen was surely him. If nothing else, he'd fulfill the sexual ache she'd carried for far too long. "Bear in mind, if our scandal is known, the potential backlash might bar you from your goal of obtaining that coveted seat."

"Of course." His hot, moist breath feathered along her neck. "If you and I are talking an affair, there are other more pleasurable payoffs for me than money or social standing. I shall find my own way into making a difference. In a country where the Peerage does much more scandalous things, I'm confident I won't have trouble finding the path."

"Smart man." Maggie's heartbeat raced through her veins. It throbbed in her fingertips in time to the need pulsing between her thighs. *What would his cock feel like pulsing there instead? I have to follow through on the lark.* She lifted a hand and cupped the back of his neck, her fingers furrowing through the silky hair at his collar. "Shall we seal the accord with a kiss? After all, nothing is decided unless you are skilled in that."

"Ah, then you will be pleasantly surprised." He lowered his face to hers, upside down in her position, and barely brushed his lips to hers before pulling away. "But for today, I'm afraid I must leave you wondering." He straightened and stepped from the bench. "There should be some mystery in the beginning to ensure you'll give chase."

Oh, he would be a challenge. Flutters filled her stomach. Maggie stood and hoped he didn't notice her wobbling knees or that the hardened buds of her nipples poked at her dress. "As much as I would love to start this grand affair tonight, I'm afraid I already have dinner plans." If he thought he'd have the upper hand in this venture, he could think again.

Stephen came around the bench and offered her his arm, lifting a dark brow when she swept her glance to the obvious bulge in his breeches. "It pains me to hear of the delay, but I am content to wait." He winked as she slipped her hand into the crook of his elbow. "Thinking about what will eventually occur makes the actual act sweeter."

"Very well." Could he feel the shake of her hand or hear the tremble in her voice as they walked? After all, it had been eight years since she'd indulged in relations with a man. "I expect to see you bright and early tomorrow morning during my usual ride. With Amanda, of course." How would he handle an added stumbling block?

"Why? I thought the point of an affair was for both participants to be alone when they embark upon it." A faint trace of annoyance rang in his voice. "And we'd settled the fact I'm not after Amanda any longer."

"We did. Perhaps I'll need her to chaperone *me*." She started them in motion along the path. Let him think what he wanted. The coming days should be every bit as thrilling as she'd imagined.

Chapter Four

Stephen yawned, blinked, and gave the sun-bathed world around him a general grin. *So this is what the English countryside before eight a.m. looks like.* Dew sparkled on the summer grass like diamonds while cheery birdsong greeted him from roadside trees and shrubs. Odd he noticed things of that ilk now. Perhaps it was the clean air clearing the smog from his brain.

Not that he wasn't accustomed to rising early. Mostly, he spent his waking moments behind a desk at his office, and the times he wasn't working he enjoyed at a club or entertaining in his London townhouse. Today, all thoughts of either seemed far away and vastly unimportant. His gaze jogged ahead, but it wasn't the idyllic scenery he admired this time. The straight line of Lady Parker's back and the slight flare of her hips captured his attention.

A man could easily become accustomed to such a sight.

"I don't understand why you needed me to accompany you on your morning ride, Aunt Margaret. I'd much rather spend this time sleeping or planning my wardrobe." Amanda's whine cut through the tranquil morning.

Or what would have been a tranquil morning if not for the young woman's complaining. What had he been about, trying to trick himself into thinking a courtship with the chit would be a good idea? Thank God for the advent of Margaret. He must have been mad to even briefly consider such a plan. After telling Maggie of his wish to gain a seat in Parliament, he'd felt peaceful, as if speaking it aloud to her had confirmed the desire, and though he was still no better off in that regard than he'd been two days ago, his future looked bright.

"And I'd prefer to ride astride, but sometimes we all must suffer disappointments in the face of more important things—like spending time together." The peacock feather on Maggie's bonnet bobbed with the motion of her horse.

Stephen's mind tripped over her words. What he wouldn't give to witness her riding astride with a prime bit of horseflesh between her thighs. Would her skirts flare around her to reveal the shapely line of her legs? What a sight that would be.

"There is nothing to do here; no one to talk to." Amanda's continued vocalization stabbed at his fantasy. "Plus, Mr. Tarkington is here for me, yet you are cheating me of time with him by talking of equine troubles."

Maggie's sigh, no doubt a sure sign of an impending dressing down, drifted back to Stephen. "There are other males in the area who are much better for you than Mr. Tarkington, and closer to your own age and temperament. If you can manage to pretend to enjoy yourself this morning, I promise to order another two gowns when the dressmaker comes by this afternoon."

"Gowns are nice, Aunt, but why can I not have *him*? I brought him here." The whine grew more pronounced, jarring through Stephen's brain.

"No, I suspect you wheedled him into coming along with you, and he is not a pet. Don't forget, I've known you since you were a babe. You have a proclivity for wrapping yourself around a male's little finger."

"He came willingly enough." Amanda glanced over her shoulder at Stephen, her expression sullen. Then she just as quickly looked ahead.

"I'm sure he did, and now I'm also sure he realizes what an enormous lapse in judgment that was. Thank goodness he did the right thing and delivered you here without incident."

"True, ... not skilled in... flirting." The *clop clop* of the horses' hooves mangled her mumble.

Stephan glared at the girl's back. Good Lord, she'd been flirting with him in the coach to Surrey? He stifled a snicker. Obviously, she needed pointers since he'd thought she had been possessed of muscle spasms in the face.

"Proper young ladies should never converse about a gentleman's flirting skills in public. And since you will apparently persist in talking about him, the question that remains is do you want him for more than the novelty of your first conquest?" Maggie peered at Stephen as well, except she gave him a tiny wink before returning her attention to her niece.

"I might."

"Well, that is your prerogative, but he also needs to want to be with you as well. Do keep in mind he's vastly older than you, and once he gains his dotage—which could be soon, you don't know what the future holds—you'll still be tied to him in the eyes of the law should you two marry. Is that how you'd like to waste the most vibrant years of your life—waiting for Mr. Tarkington to die before you're free?"

"I suppose not. He *is* old. Your age even, but he's here and I haven't met any other men."

Damnation, she makes me sound as if I have one foot in the grave already. On the other hand, the fact she'd cast him aside so fast in her affections wouldn't have boded well had they tried to make a match of it. He shook his head as relief shuddered through him.

Amanda looked at her aunt. "Please, will you introduce me to some of the county's eligible gentlemen?"

"I will, and you're young. Don't rush life." Maggie's head bobbed. "Now, let's talk gowns, shall we? I'm hosting a ball to introduce you to local society in a few days and you'll need something exquisite."

"Will there be dancing?"

"Yes, but do remember, this will not be a lavish affair as you might encounter in London."

Stephen rolled his eyes and coughed to remind them of his presence. They ignored him. He shrugged, glad that he rode behind the women and therefore remained out of the direct conversation of female trappings. Truth be told, he'd rather watch Maggie. Today, she wore an emerald riding habit that clung to her body and displayed her curves to advantage. Scuffed brown boots peeked from beneath the hem as she sat on the sidesaddle, her back straight and proud. As he slacked off on the reins, he revisited their meeting from yesterday.

What had begun as a test of her mettle had rapidly surprised him. He'd had no intention of teasing her like he had during their talk, but once he'd caught wind of her wish for a scandal, he couldn't help himself. The more he'd breathed in her lilac scent then experienced that first touch of creamy, soft skin, the further he'd wanted to go. Each time he'd caressed her, she'd encouraged him. It had only been natural to slide his fingers over her breast, yet that mere brush of his fingers over her nipple hadn't cooled his ardor.

Lady Maggie Parker captivated his mind and inflamed his body. He craved more interaction, especially since she'd put him off last night—not that she hadn't had a legitimate dinner engagement. She had gone on to keep the appointment while Alfred took Amanda on a tour of the grounds and gardens, much to her consternation. Once concluded, Amanda shut herself in her room, and Maggie didn't return to the manor until late. He'd assumed if she'd wanted to start an affair on the grand scale she'd hinted at that, she'd want to start immediately.

Cheeky woman. Stephen grinned. She knew exactly how to fan those flames she'd created. The chase was indeed part of the excitement. He counted himself lucky that she'd accepted him for her gambit with nothing else but his word to go by. He appreciated her trust.

"Mr. Tarkington, will you be contributing to this conversation, or shall I send you back to the house for the remainder of your wool gathering?" Maggie's strident question slashed through his thoughts with an urgency that made him think she'd been trying for his attention for some minutes.

Stephen pulled sharply on the reins to avoid plowing his mount between her horse and Amanda's. He glanced at Maggie and startled at the hunger in her eyes. Did she know he thought of her? Could she see it in his expression? Did her thoughts rest on him as well? "I beg your pardon, Lady Parker. My attention was... elsewhere."

"So I can see." Maggie's horse danced in place then maneuvered backward, by its own will or her design, he couldn't say, until one of her legs brushed his. Heat jumped up his limb and lodged in his groin.

"Did you need my opinion for something in particular? The last I checked, you were engaged in talks with Miss Manning about gods know what kind of feminine hullabaloo." His horse blew out a breath, and Stephen tightened his grip on the reins, keeping his animal still.

"That line of discussion has run its course. I had asked if you were able to enjoy much riding in London. After all, you appear quite fit, so if you do not, I wonder how you keep trim." Her blue eyes twinkled, but she gave no other outward sign she enjoyed herself at his expense. Those eyes, no matter that they mocked him, had the power to melt him with its heat.

"Mr. Tarkington was walking quite briskly when I first met him." Amanda's interruption did little to cut the rising tension between him and Maggie.

He glanced at Amanda. "I was, thank you for reminding me."

"I wouldn't mind walking the estate with you." Her eyelashes fluttered but she kept her gaze downcast.

Maggie clucked. "Oh, darling, when will you have the time, what with all the fittings and other last-minute preparations for your debut?"

"But, Aunt, you said—"

Not willing to listen to more complaints, Stephen cleared his throat. "Perhaps another time, Miss Manning."

"I think my aunt is keeping us apart for her own evil plans."

Stephen glanced sharply at Maggie's face, but she gave nothing away. Had they been so obvious in their attraction? "Interesting."

"No, none of this is interesting, and neither are you if you cannot entertain me with dashing stories or something that makes me heart pound."

"I apologize. I had not thought to come prepared to entertain." The chit's behavior was rapidly growing out of hand.

She pouted. "I'm bored, Auntie." The young lady's attention wavered and focused on an approaching coach.

Stephen touched the brim of his beaver pelt that and leaned closer to Maggie, taking full advantage of the lapse. "How astute of you to notice my form, Lady Parker. While I do ride on occasion, horseflesh is not my preferred mount of choice."

A pretty blush stained Maggie's cheeks, but she didn't lose her composure. With her voice as low as his, she volleyed, "Ah, then you must lead quite an active social life if that is how you find your exercise. Perhaps I should rethink my own plans if you've previously been put through your paces by others."

Damnation. His attempt at innuendo had provoked the wrong sort of reaction. "I do apologize. I'm very particular in that regard, and haven't found a mount to interest me in that way for a while." Why couldn't the chit move off and let him explain in a better manner?

The corners of Maggie's mouth tipped upward yet she kept her attention fixed on the oncoming carriage. "We will revisit this conversation in a moment." With one flick of her wrist, she maneuvered her horse near Amanda's. "You are in luck, my girl.

Your first introduction into country society will come sooner than I thought."

Stephen's pulse increased. If the newcomer kept Amanda busy for a few minutes, then he'd have Maggie all to himself. What a delightful prospect. "Who approaches?"

"That's Squire Collins' traveling coach." In a low voice to them both she said, "It's the squire's eldest son, David."

As the conveyance rolled to a halt, the window glass slid down and a blond-haired youth stuck his head out. "Lady Parker! How goes it?"

She nodded at the young man. "Very well, thank you, and welcome home, David. How are you? We've missed you around here since you've been away at school."

"Excellent. I'm freshly free from Cambridge and ready to find adventure."

Maggie's lips twitched. "Ah. A good prerogative to have. Perhaps you'd enjoy stretching your legs after your journey?" Maggie slid from her mount and looped the reins over the pommel. "Dismount, if you please Amanda, and smooth the wrinkles from your skirt." She waited long enough for her niece to follow instructions. "It's advantageous for us to meet you right now, David."

Stephen watched the proceedings with more than a little interest. As the youth bounded out of the coach—tall, lean and with an expression akin to a man who has just been granted a pardon—Stephen grinned. Perhaps the young man would be just the thing to distract Amanda from any more designs.

"I'm glad to be home." The young man, probably not older than twenty-two, rushed across the road and took one of Lady Parker's hands in both of his. "And who are your guests? Father didn't warn me there'd be a pretty young lady in residence; otherwise, I would have come home sooner."

Amanda blushed to the roots of her hair while Maggie merely raised an eyebrow. The chit had not given him such a reaction when he'd met her. This was all to the good. Stephen dismounted and strode to the gathering, intent on displacing the boy from Maggie's hand.

"Good morning, sir." He narrowed his eyes as a thread of jealousy climbed his spine. "I'm Stephen Tarkington, visiting from London, an acquaintance of Lady Parker's niece, Miss Amanda Tarkington." He stuck out a hand. The boy had no choice but to leave Maggie alone to shake his hand.

"David Collins, at your service," Though he heartily shook Stephen's hand, his gaze had strayed to Amanda.

Maggie cleared her throat. "Thank you for assuming the introductions, Mr. Tarkington." She put a hand on Amanda's arm and drew her niece closer to David. "Mr. Collins, this is my niece, Miss Manning. I believe you two are of an age. Perhaps you'd enjoy a quick visit here in the lane and then do us the honor of coming to tea later this afternoon?"

"Thank you, Lady Parker. I'm sure my parents will appreciate your invitation." His eyes widened when Amanda gave him a pretty smile.

"Nonsense. I always enjoy visiting with your mother and sister. In any event, we're all invited to your estate tomorrow evening for a rout, to celebrate your homecoming." Maggie turned to her niece. "Mr. Tarkington and I will keep an eye on you just down the lane as we walk the horses."

Stephen bit back his grin. Not that it mattered. Amanda only had eyes for the golden-haired new arrival. How fortuitous. He fell into step with Maggie as they returned to the horses. "You are very skilled in moving people into the positions you want them to be."

"I'm efficient, yes."

He loosed his grin. Giddy from being alone in her company, he decided to play his intentions to the hilt. Would she go along, or would she take offense? "Does your efficiency carry over into manipulating positions in a bedroom setting as well?"

"Ah, that depends on the man and the circumstances, doesn't it?" She drew a gloved hand along her horse's neck. "I must warn you that the importance doesn't lie so much in the position than how the man employs his member." The glance she slid him brimmed with suggestion. "How skilled are you in that regard?"

Heat lanced through his body and pressed his cock against his riding breeches. What luck! Not only had she taken to his suggestive teasing, but she continued the banter. She was very different than any woman he'd ever known, and that stimulated him. "I believe in this instance, actions will speak much louder than words. Perhaps you should tell me when you'll be available for a private performance."

"While that would be a good start for an affair, I believe I did ask for a kiss to gauge your skill and commit your promise." She offered no protest when her horse meandered to the side of the road and began eating at the clumps of grass there. The other two horses followed. "If you'll recall, you cheated me out of that yesterday."

"I did, but it pleases me to know it bothered you." He trailed after Maggie as she stepped into the grass and moved toward a blackberry bramble.

"Perhaps the time for a revelation is upon us... unless you've told me a fib and don't possess the skill you've hinted at." She trailed a fingertip along the ribbon beneath her chin that held her bonnet in place.

Stephen swallowed past the sudden dryness in his throat. The woman was trouble enough with her plain speaking and forward thinking. How would she act in the bedroom? Would she assume the lead there as well? Would he let her? "What about your niece?" He glanced down the lane where Amanda still chatted with the eager David. Neither appeared to notice anyone beyond themselves.

"You know how self-absorbed young people are." Maggie laid a gloved hand on his sleeve. "Plenty of time to steal a kiss that will prompt me to assign a rendezvous point." She gripped his sleeve and tugged him toward the hedgerow. "How badly do you want to progress this scandal?"

"Very much so." He allowed her the lead until they were out of eyesight of the younger couple. Then he caught her in an embrace, sliding one arm firmly around her waist while the other supported her shoulders. "Perhaps even more than you."

Maggie's eyes flashed brilliant blue fire as she smiled, her hands moving steadily up his chest. "That remains to be seen."

"Allow me to help you sort out the tangle." Stephen lowered his lips to hers. Soft and pliant, they cushioned his and welcomed him with gentle warmth. He pulled away for the space of a heartbeat in order to peer into her eyes. She nodded and pressed her body closer to his. He settled her more firmly into his arms and applied himself to the kiss.

Her scent enveloped him, and her hands crept behind his neck, tugging him closer. He nibbled at the corners of her mouth and explored her silky lips, still holding off deepening their meeting for the simple fact he wanted to enjoy tasting her. She was sweet as honey, and a hint of tea clung to her tongue. With consummate care, he stroked his tongue along her bottom lip, tracing it, teasing back and forth, and acquainting himself with every nuance of that bit of flesh. When she uttered a breathy moan, he suckled that lip and nipped it before releasing it to begin the same assault on the upper portion of her exquisite mouth.

What he wouldn't do to spend hours kissing her, experiencing her lips on his skin or closing around his member. Heat raced through his groin, and he groaned against her mouth.

She half-broke the kiss, but only enough to whisper, "Dear Lord, I need more."

He loved how voracious she was, with a passion that matched his. Stephen held Maggie close. His hand moved to the small of her back and he trapped her against his body, hoping for some relief for his aching cock. When there was none to be had, he thrust his tongue into her mouth, seeking hers, needing the carnal satisfaction of entering her immediately. She tightened her hold on his neck and stood on tiptoe, meeting him stroke for stroke. Warm and satiny, her tongue slid against his in a sensual, all-consuming dance that set fire to his blood and had the power to turn him inside out. He wanted to knock the bonnet from her head and bury his fingers in her hair. He craved even closer contact, needed to feel her skin, possess her body the way he plundered her mouth.

But not here, not like this.

Wrenching away, his breathing labored, he trailed his lips down the silky column of her throat along her rapid pulse. "Maggie, you must know how much I want you. Delay at this point is ridiculous."

"I do know, but I need more confirmation." She slid a hand between them and cupped his manhood through his breeches. "Now, I'm certain."

He thought he'd spend right there behind the blackberry bushes as she rubbed her fingers along his length, traced the outline of his balls and then returned to stroke the front of his shaft, her fingertips centimeters from its head. "When..." He groaned when she repeated the action. He shuddered. "When shall we meet? I cannot survive this teasing."

"I completely understand." Her sigh feathered across his jaw. She licked her kiss-swollen lips and moved away, her steps shaky. "After the rout at Squire Collins' home tomorrow evening. As much as I want you in my bed beforehand, I'm afraid my time is committed with Amanda."

"What about this evening?" God, he sounded desperate, but it couldn't be helped.

"I'm having a few guests over to meet Amanda for a cozy supper. I have no notion of when I'll be free." Her gaze faltered and she stared at the ground. "Had I known of you beforehand..."

Damnation! How the hell would he survive the remainder of this day and the next away from her company? Stephen shoved a hand through his hair. "Fate has a way of playing the bitch, but I'll take what I can get."

Maggie nodded, her eyes wide and dark with desire. "Stephen, I—"

"Aunt Margaret? Where are you?" Amanda's call shattered Maggie's words to the point he couldn't understand what she'd said. "Mr. Collins is just leaving."

"I'm coming." Maggie hurried around the hedgerow while Stephen followed at a more sedate pace. She dispensed with a few more pleasantries then the young man ducked into the carriage. It rumbled down the lane and was soon out of sight.

Thankfully, Stephen's horse had drifted over the grass, so he used the excuse of guiding the animal back onto the lane to hide his engorged cock. Willpower alone kept him from glancing at Maggie while she pulled her horse to a fair-sized rock and flung herself into her saddle. Her skirts fluttered up and treated him to a glimpse of a nicely turned ankle and slender calf before she arranged the material over her limbs. Damnation she was a looker. Feeling eyes upon him, he glanced up and caught Amanda's gaze over the back of his horse. "I apologize for the delay. Upon stretching her legs, your aunt got her foot caught in a rabbit's hole. It took me considerable moments in the attempt to free her." The lie tripped off his tongue as if he'd spent a lifetime disassembling.

Amanda narrowed her gaze. "That must have been a large hole."

"Indeed." His spine tingled with chills. The chit *knew*, he'd bet money on it.

"How nice that you took the time to keep my aunt company, Mr. Tarkington. I'm sure she appreciates the chance to talk to someone near her own age as her behavior since she's been widowed has been less than socially pleasing. Most men shy away from being seen in her company."

While Stephen gaped, rendered speechless at the slur, Amanda brought her horse close to Maggie's. "Aunt Margaret, did you thrash about on the ground in your quest to be free of the hole? Your habit is wrinkled, and your face is flushed as if you struggled."

"Don't be silly." Maggie wheeled her mount around. Sure enough, a flush pinked her cheeks. "I find I'm rather fatigued at the moment, Amanda. Please mount so we can conclude our outing."

After sundown, once Maggie, Alfred and Amanda were committed to dinner with Maggie's guests, Stephen popped into a local tavern and occupied a stool at the battered and scarred bar. Sometimes a man just needed to be with other men for the sheer purpose of maintaining his sanity. He'd declined the invitation to join Maggie and her family, not trusting his discretion to be in her company yet keep his hands to himself.

"One pint, mate." The barkeep plunked down a tankard. Foam slipped over the rim and sloshed down the side of the mug.

"Thank you." Stephen took a hearty swig. "I have a question. What do you know of Lady Parker? She owns the property not far from here."

"Aye, I know who she is. We *all* know." The older gentleman leaned a fat hip against the bar. "There's nothing that Lady Parker loves more than a scandal."

Then the rumors her brother had hinted about were true. "Oh? Why's that?" He nodded as a balding, portly fellow occupied the stool next to his.

"That one's a hoyden." The newcomer signaled for his own pint. "Started after Baron Parker died. He was always the sickly type and much older, but once she put him in the ground, she changed her life. Never wanted to stay indoors. Never wanted to be a proper lady. Did everything she could outside, on horseback or walking the property, and more than once she was caught swimming in men's trousers or worse." The man glanced furtively about the area. "Once, I heard a man spied her naked."

Stephen sucked down another mouthful of ale even as his chest constricted. He didn't take issue with her penchant for scandal, but she needed to understand the possibility men could catch her at it. That didn't sit well. "Do her scandals revolve around affairs?" Though he'd not shared anything except a kiss with Maggie, the thought of her with other men made his stomach churn.

"Nah." The barkeep gave Stephen's companion a tankard. "Many men have tried to court her. Eventually, they just gave up. She's too high-spirited for respectable men to take on and too independent for the rogues."

"I see, but she has a sharp tongue and a sharper mind. No one is able to look past her shortcomings?"

"Not if they know what's good for them."

"She does seem like the type of woman to give a merry chase." He grinned over his next sip. "Do you have any pointers if a man did want to take her on?"

Every man in his vicinity burst into laughter.

The farmer beside him slapped a palm on the bar. "Good luck to you, mate. She's one riddle no man should try and solve." He took a swig of his ale. "Just remember, if you want Lady Parker to take an interest in you, make sure you dare her to do something. She never backs down from a challenge. Many a cocky youth has lost a horse to her."

Stephen nodded and tucked that bit of information away.

The barkeep smirked and rubbed a rag down a length of the counter. "If you're looking for marriage, Lady Parker isn't that kind. She's too wild to settle down again. I don't think marriage agreed with her in the first place."

"Good thing I'm not looking for a wife." He stared into his drink as emptiness yawned in the pit of his stomach. Why did that statement depress him?

Chapter Five

Stephen hummed to himself as he put the final adjustments to his cravat. Alfred had lent him the services of his valet as he hadn't brought his, intending to make do for a short stay in Surrey yet his man had packed enough clothes for a longer stay. He'd accepted the loaned services with gratitude as his dress jacket was quite a bear to don by himself, but he saw to his cravat. There was a certain satisfaction in knowing the exquisite turn of a knot or creation of a design was by his own hand. Plus, Alfred's man had coaxed Stephen's hair into fashionable windblown waves, and Stephen had paid him handsomely based on that skill alone. He wanted to look his best tonight for Maggie. Nothing would come between him and starting the affair. He'd waited long enough. Tonight, her body would belong to him. He'd apply himself to knowing the rest of the woman soon after.

A knock sounded on his door. He bade the person entrance and turned when the door opened. Alfred stood in its frame. "You're looking dapper this evening, Stephen."

"Thank you, as do you. Thank you as well for extending an invitation for me."

"You can thank the squire. He jumped at the chance to have another male at his party, a male who wasn't young or interested in prowling for debutantes."

"I have no interest in debutantes." He grabbed a ruby stickpin from the bureau top and pushed the sharp end through the snowy folds of his cravat. "It's been quite a long time since I've felt such a thrill to be with a woman." Finished with his toilette, he regarded Alfred, who also wore the requisite dark evening clothes. "I trust I have your approval where your sister is concerned?"

"Since she has told me of her plans, yes." Alfred fiddled with his spectacles. "Has she outright told *you* she wishes to enter into an affair?"

"Oh, yes, in words as in deeds."

"Please, keep that knowledge to yourself. She is my sister, after all." Alfred held up a hand. "I don't see the harm in a dalliance—unless you plan to engage her heart and leave her in emotional ruin once you return to London." He shot an accusatory glance at Stephen. "You are planning to return, correct?"

The question stole the edge from Stephen's excitement. "Eventually, yes. I'll admit I hadn't thought that far ahead as an affair wasn't my original plan, but my business will need me sooner than later." He frowned. He'd told his office that he'd not be away for more than a week—a fortnight if everything went well. Including travel, he'd currently been gone for four days. Obviously, the plan to pursue Amanda had been thwarted before it began, replaced by a different, much more satisfying one. Once he bedded Maggie, would he want to leave her so soon? Usually, if he took a mistress, both he and she were located in London. If he left Surrey, what were the chances he'd see Maggie after that? Would distance crush the heat developing between them?

Stephen rubbed a hand along his recently shaved jaw. "I promise to be aware of your sister's sensibilities. If she weren't a willing participant, I'd leave her be." But she was willing. Even now, more than a day later, he swore he still felt the heat of her hand on his cock. His member twitched. "In fact, I wouldn't mind knowing her beyond the carnal. I've never met a woman with such a zest for life."

"I'll trust you and your word as a gentleman." Alfred leaned a shoulder against the doorframe and crossed his arms over his chest. "See here, though. Mags is high strung and looking for scandal, but she has a good heart. She hasn't been quite the same since she lost Jamie, so please, have a care. If it doesn't feel like a lark anymore, I want you to beg off."

"Losing a spouse does change a person's outlook." He cast about for his top hat, finally locating it on a wingback chair in one corner of the room.

"Maggie hasn't told you her history then. Jamie was her *son*. He died at the age of five while riding a pony."

"I didn't know." Stephen closed his fingers around the hat's brim. His gut clenched. "Your sister and I haven't had a moment alone for any sort of discussion—personal or otherwise." Of course, he hadn't shared his past either, an oversight he should address soon.

Alfred straightened, his expression closed and shadowed with sadness. "Personally, I believe Jamie's death affected Mags more than she's let on. I suspect that's why she engages in scandal—as a way to forget, or perhaps as a way to gain the attention she wasn't allowed to have during that time. Baron Parker was a very private, quiet fellow. In keeping with tradition, he didn't show his grief outwardly, and in retrospect, I don't guess he allowed Mags to do so either."

Stephen's heart hurt for her loss while his mind screamed with questions. Was her inherent confidence merely a mask? If it was, would pushing her to start the affair be considered taking advantage? And did her internalizing her grief motivate her passions? "My condolences. She never said anything." He knew exactly what she went through. "I lost my first wife and only child during childbirth. It's not something you forget; no matter how hard you fill your life with other things."

"Quite all right. It was a long time ago." Alfred closed the distance and clasped Stephen's shoulder. "If you can bring her happiness, and she enjoys herself while she's with you, then it's all to the good. If she doesn't turn you off the property afterward, consider yourself lucky."

"I shall bear that in mind." He cleared his throat, anxious to move the conversation into safer subjects. "How far away is the squire's estate?"

"Nearly an hour."

"If I could ask a favor?" Stephen slid on his gloves.

"Certainly."

"Could you contrive for your sister and me to be in one carriage and the rest of you to take a different conveyance?" He raised an eyebrow, hoping the other man understood.

Alfred grinned and nodded. "Of course. If you happen to have an issue with your cravat, such a delay would let my carriage depart first. You'll have Billy the groom with you as driver." He winked. "I'll arrange for you to have the smaller carriage. It's cozier."

"Thank you." Stephen held out his hand and gave Alfred's a vigorous shake once he'd clasped it. "You're a good man, Alfred."

"I am until Mags gets wind of my involvement in this scheme. Then we're both in the drink. See that she doesn't." He strode to the door. "Good luck. If she wasn't so determined to keep your relationship to an affair, I'd push for a proper courtship."

"Except your sister doesn't do anything proper, does she?"

"No, but there are always exceptions to any rule." Alfred nodded. "Good luck to you though."

"Thank you." Stephen frowned for long moments after Alfred had quit the room. With every *on dit* he discovered about Maggie, the more he wanted to know her beyond a physical relationship, yet marriage? He hadn't excelled in that area to date. Why should he hope the third time would be different?

He wasn't looking for a lifetime, and even if he was, Maggie was not. These were the cards fate had dealt. He'd play them and not complain. Until then, he intended to enjoy himself regardless of the little niggles of doubt.

Good grief.

"I do not understand why it took you a quarter of an hour to decide on a stick pin." Maggie's annoyance oozed from her as if it had a life of its own. "We're completely off schedule and will arrive late. I did want to witness Amanda's first steps into the adult world."

"Never fear. Billy has assured me he can easily make up the time." Stephen bit back his grin as he handed her into the closed carriage. He'd invented a tale regarding his poor choice of stickpins, which precipitated him hunting for another one which would better compliment his attire. In the end, he'd chosen a square-cut emerald. Just as they'd stepped onto the drive, a steady rain had begun to fall and brought a slight cooling to the air. The perfect setting for a seduction. "I'm sure Amanda will have many other such moments."

"Oh, bother. I don't want to hear it, you vain ruffian." She gathered her skirting and arranged it around her legs. "If I didn't know better, I'd say you contrived this whole situation in order to have me compromised."

"Well, that is a crucial element in having an affair." His pulse increased while he waited for her to settle. The opportunity to verbally spar with her couldn't be missed. "Not to mention, when you make your entrance, every eye will be on you, which is as it should be. Young people have their place in society, but I'd lay odds folks would rather see a woman of character."

"Or of older years?"

"Some women grow more attractive as they age." He clambered into the carriage and sat across from her, facing forward on the tooled leather benches. "You look quite dashing this evening."

He grinned. Her gown of robin's egg blue was shot with gold thread and set off her pale skin to perfection. His gaze fell to the low-cut bodice that displayed the tops of her creamy breasts. He couldn't wait to sample them. "I'm hard pressed to escort you to the party tonight when everything within me screams to spirit you off and have my wicked way."

"You, Mr. Tarkington, are laying on the compliments thick tonight." One of her knees bumped his across the narrow aisle. Tendrils of need ebbed from the spot to culminate in his cock. "Yet, I thank you. It's a rare occurrence that I receive notice anymore."

As soon as the footman closed the carriage door, the conveyance lurched into motion. "Then you must endeavor to go to more parties. I'm certain there are many men in Surrey who'd gladly rush to your side." He removed his top hat and laid it carefully on the seat next to him.

Maggie tossed her head. "I doubt that. If it was true, wouldn't they have already declared their interest?"

"Perhaps they are shy." He removed his gloves and tucked them into a pocket of his jacket.

"I've been widowed for eight years. Some intrepid men have attempted to court me, but they weren't up to snuff." A wistful note crept into her voice. "It's all well and good to have Alfred as company, but there are only certain topics I can discuss with my brother."

Did that mean she searched for a long-term companion? "Perhaps they do not know what to do while in your company."

"I find that hard to believe. Besides, you are the first man in years who I've actually wanted to spend time with—for longer than a dinner partner that is."

"Ah, ahead of the pack, am I?" He drew closed the heavy, black curtains of each window on the side nearest to him and then did the same on her side. "The knowledge gives some comfort."

"Why is that?" Her eyes glittered in the lantern-lit darkness. Did the secured privacy of the carriage set her pulse racing?

"While the addlepated men of Surrey might be too intimidated to do you proud, I am very much up for the challenge." Stephen worked at keeping his breathing even. It wouldn't do to rush the seduction, but damn, the prospect of sitting calmly across from her without touching tried his patience.

"I see." She clasped her gloved fingers in her lap. "Did you arrange for us to be alone in this carriage? When I talked with Alfie earlier, he'd told me we could all fit into the large coach."

"I did." He had no reason to lie. "What better way to begin your affair than being naughty in a closed, private carriage." Before he could change his mind, he resituated himself onto the bench seat next to her. "I intend to be more than a bit naughty tonight."

The steady rain beating onto the carriage roof was the only sound between them for several seconds. Stephen held her gaze, dark in the dim light, and then dared to take her hand. He ran his fingers along the inside of her arm until he reached the edge of her elbow-length glove. She trembled beneath his fingertips, and he enjoyed knowing that a simple touch could affect her. "Say the word and the journey to Squire Carson's estate will pass in a lust-filled haze."

"I would like that." She turned toward him, her knee touching his. "You've teased me enough. Any more delay will diminish my reasoning power."

Stephen encouraged the glove down her arm and pulled it from her hand, dropping it into her lap. "Perhaps you don't need to think. Only feel." He lifted her arm to his lips and nipped a line of gentle bites down the inside. Her skin was soft and scented of lilacs, and he couldn't get enough. When he reached her wrist, he ran the tip of his tongue over her pulse point before going lower to ply her palm with kisses. "What would you have me do, Maggie? How do you enjoy being touched?"

"It's been such a long time, I scarcely know." She leaned toward him, her lips slightly parted. "Perhaps I should give myself over into your care."

"Dangerous words, my lady." He smoothed his palm up her bared arm, over the capped sleeve and then onward to traverse her shoulder. Soft and heated, her skin fairly cried out for his attention. "But if you wish it, I'd be happy to take advantage."

"It's not an advantage if I ask you to." Maggie pressed herself against him, and her leg rubbed against his. Any closer and she'd be in his lap. She dropped a hand to his thigh, her fingers perilously close to his hardening cock. "Kiss me, Stephen. Touch me. Make me forget my name for the moment."

"Gladly." Could she hear the wild pounding of his heart? He slid a hand around her shoulders and plied tiny, nibbling kisses along the column of her throat. When she lifted her chin, he took advantage of the greater access by licking a path along her jaw. "God, I cannot get enough of you."

"Good thing I've offered you *carte blanche*." She moved a hand up his thigh and drew a finger along his crotch. His cock twitched at her touch, and he shifted to give her more room to play. "The gossips would verbally hang me, but I need to feel your manhood in my hand. I cannot wait." She trailed her fingers over the front of his trousers then fumbled with the top button.

Stephen bit back a moan. Her unabashed exploration fanned his desire and sent blood rushing into his loins. "All in good time. There is a certain process for seduction." The carriage lurched and threw her half on his lap. "How fortuitous." He wrapped his arms around her waist and claimed her lips.

A soft sigh escaped, and Maggie twined her hands behind his neck. Her mouth, pliant beneath his, opened. It was her tongue that thrust first, tangled with his and then retreated, waiting until he pursued before fencing with his again.

Stephen's willpower cracked. He needed to touch her skin, feel her body, see her womanly curves else he'd explode. Never had a woman teased him like Maggie did; never had a woman taunted him on every level as fast as she had. Pulling away, he peppered soft kisses over her face—her cheeks, the tip of her nose, her closed eyelids. Every new kiss brought him closer to bliss and her scent floated around him, making him drunk on her essence. He ran his fingers up her back, the stiffness of her stays providing texture beneath the satin. Finding the abbreviated row of buttons above the high waist of her gown, he worried them from their holes and was rewarded when the gown's bodice sagged around her bosom.

"Now we begin the next step." He dipped his hands inside the gown and cupped her breasts, teasing her hardened shift-covered nipples with his thumbs while he nibbled her lips. "I've waited for this moment since the rose arbor."

Maggie gripped his elbows and threw her head back. "Oh Stephen, yes."

Just as he lowered his lips to the swell of one breast, the carriage lurched again, more violent this time, and the unmistakable crack of a wheel breaking intruded into the moment. Stephen lifted his head as the carriage came to an abrupt halt then swayed. A swift knock on the door followed seconds later. "Damnation." He eased Maggie onto the bench beside him. "I shall return shortly. Stay inside where it's dry."

Cursing the interruption, Stephen opened the door and climbed down to stand beside Billy on the wet, muddy road. Desultory rain dampened his head. "What happened?" He closed the door to give Maggie privacy. No one but him got the honor of looking upon her in such an undone state.

"The puddles hid a hole. It's hard to see through the rain. I went over it and one of the back wheels busted." Billy knelt at the rear left wheel. The rain had soaked his natty wool coat. "It's broken and the rim's come off."

Stephen wiped at the rain on his forehead. "Are you carrying a replacement?"

"Not on this vehicle. Too small."

"How far away are we from Squire Carson's?" He glanced up and down the darkened road. Nothing stirred except eddies in the puddles from the raindrops. Somewhere in the distance, a frog croaked. Since he'd been occupied with Maggie, he had no idea how long they'd traveled.

"'Bout halfway there. Got another few miles to go yet." Billy stood and brushed at the wet spots on his trousers. "What should we do?"

"Why don't you take the horse, go back to the Parker estate, and bring a replacement wheel here. Barring that, you'll need to go to the squire's and retrieve Mr. Manning's coach."

Billy pulled the brim of his cap lower over his eyes. "Will you and Lady Parker be all right if I leave you here?"

Honor demanded Stephen go himself, but as he wasn't familiar with the country roads, especially in the dark, he opted to send the groom. "Of course. I'd protect Lady Parker with my life."

The young groom nodded. Water dripped from the brim of his cap. "I'll be as quick as I can." He walked to the horse and began undoing the leads that attached it to the equipage. "Foul weather, eh? Best not stand around in this mess long, sir. It'll ruin your evening clothes."

Stephen's gut churned at the huge differences in their positions. "Right you are." He dug in a trouser pocket and withdrew a guinea. "Here's a little something for your trouble." He flipped the coin in the boy's direction. "I'll give you another if you make the trip quick." It was a foul night indeed to be riding. His neck heated with shame. He should be the one going for help, yet his own selfish interest kept him from offering.

"I'll try my best." Billy pocketed the money and then succeeded in freeing the horse. "I'm off then."

"Be careful on the roads." He waited until Billy had mounted the horse and swung it around before he opened the carriage door and climbed in. Maggie's dark gaze immediately landed on him. "One of the wheels is broken. Billy's gone for help." Sitting heavily on the bench opposite her once more, he closed the door. "I'm paying him handsomely for his trouble."

"You have a good heart, Stephen."

He grimaced and ran his fingers through his sopping hair. "At the moment, I feel as if it's black. I should have gone."

"And leave me here in such a state?"

Oh, she'd be the death of him with her teasing. "Would you mind helping me with the jacket? I'd rather not sit and wait in wet clothes." As he shrugged the coat from his shoulders, he turned his back to her. Fabric rustled while Maggie maneuvered into the cramped aisle. She slid the tailored garment down his arms. "Ah, thank you. Much better."

"Will you feel like shedding more clothes this evening?" She settled back onto her bench with his jacket folded beside her. "I can help with that as well."

"Cheeky woman." Stephen had no sooner shifted on his own bench when the carriage lurched again. A loud crack rent the air and the equipage tilted downward at a drunken angle. "Hellfire. I think the wheel just separated." While he reached out to make sure Maggie remained upright, the carriage jerked. Wood splintered and the backside of the vehicle slammed against the ground. The abrupt motion sent Maggie flying across the aisle. She landed on her knees, between his, with her face on intimate terms with his crotch.

"Damn. I believe the axle just gave way." He couldn't move, could scarcely breathe with Maggie so close and in such a precarious position. The gaping bodice of her gown showed the swell of her breasts, the lace of her shift clinging to the pale mounds. His mouth watered.

"This does put things into an interesting perspective." She raised her head, her gaze seeking his while both ungloved hands wrapped around his calves. "What to do?"

Obviously, she could no longer perch on the opposite seat as gravity made that impossible. Stephen swallowed. He tugged the pin from her hat. With shaking hands, he removed her beribboned and flowered headgear then stuck the pin in its crown. "Do you have an idea?" His voice sounded rough. God, despite their unorthodox plight, his need for her had grown.

Maggie took the hat from him and flung it to the floor. "Yes." She slid her hands over his thighs until she reached his waistband. "You kissed me earlier, now we'll play into my urges, and I wish to see your cock." One by one, she undid the buttons of his trousers and then, just as slowly, she pushed the fabric and small pants down until his member sprang free.

Stephen sucked in a great gulp of air as she leaned closer. *Mother of God, I'm in a spot of trouble.*

Chapter Six

Flutters filled Maggie's belly. Heat invaded her core while she feasted her eyes on his length. Here was a man who could satiate her in bed. Here was a man who could hold her in his arms and allow her to forget about the heartaches she'd experienced and make her look forward to the future... except an affair didn't mean forever. Did she want it to?

She pushed the thought away. Now was not the time. They'd need to have a serious discussion afterward. "I knew you'd be more than satisfactory." The remembrance of how big he'd felt in her hand had haunted her waking moments since that interlude by the blackberry brambles.

His rich chuckle filled the small space. "My dear, you haven't had the honor of seeing me use it."

"An oversight I plan to have rectified soon." Maggie kissed the wide head of his cock and grinned when he shuddered. "My late husband enjoyed intercourse, but he never let me pleasure him orally, at least not after the first time I attempted it, no matter how much it excited me. He had a bit of an issue with the unsanitary concept of it." She swirled her tongue around the tip and savored the earthy, salty tang of him. "What about you, Stephen? Do you harbor any such opinions?"

"No." Strain graveled the word. "Feel free to explore as much as you'd like. I won't complain." He shifted on the bench as she settled between his legs. "Your affair should be everything you've imagined."

"I'll make certain you enjoy it as well. Remember, it is an affair for us both." Maggie curled a hand around his shaft and smoothed her fingers down to the base. As she repeated the gesture, his length grew and thickened. She glanced at his face, but the darkness shadowed it too much to read his expression. "I'm glad you suggested taking a private carriage. I've wished to do this since the liberties of yesterday."

"You took me by surprise." He drew the back of one hand along her cheek. "That doesn't happen often."

"You have a compelling air about you. I couldn't resist." After licking her lips, she took him into her mouth and slid down his silky, rigid cock. Stephen remained still, almost as if he feared to move. Maggie moaned around his member; he felt so good and filled her mouth with his warm girth. Heated dampness tickled her feminine curls. Oh, what she wouldn't give to feel him in her body, rubbing against her sex to send her flying. She whimpered her need and retreated in order to suck on his tip before backing off. "More?"

"Yes." Raw demand ripped the word from his throat. He slid a hand into her upswept hair and tugged her closer. "Please."

I do so love to hear a man beg. Maggie applied herself to the task with more vigor, sucking hard on the head and then relaxing. She licked his shaft, teasing the sensitive underside near the tip, humming with pride when he thrust into her mouth. Oh, he felt good! As he hit the back of her throat, she opened wider, wishing to experience the act fully. After taking him as deep as she could, she pulled back, gently scraping his flesh with her teeth. Stephen moaned, and she repeated the action. He thrust once before he made a strangled sound and urged her off him.

"My God, Maggie, you must cease else I'll embarrass myself."

"Isn't that a good outcome?" Pleasure curled tight in her core. She wanted to drive him to the brink and watch him explode.

"Extremely, but when that eventuality occurs, it will damn well be inside you." He tucked his erection into his trousers.

A twinge of disappointment gripped her stomach. Why must he hide himself so quickly? "I'm glad I affect you so." Yet, if his words were true, wouldn't he leave his cock uncovered?

"You are more potent than you think. Now, come here so I can return the favor."

Maggie's pulse tripped into double time. Would he put his mouth on her like she'd done him? Gooseflesh raced over her skin, and she wondered at the intelligence of an affair with him. He was intense and matched her with desire. What would happen were she to abandon her thoughts and simply enjoy the scandal or let herself start to care for him? "Where?"

"My lap."

She stopped thinking, not wishing to ruin the moment, hitched up her skirts and straddled him. There was really nowhere else to go since the carriage tilted at a crazy angle. As soon as she settled, his hands were at her bodice, shoving the loose fabric down. He cupped her breasts, lifting them from the lace-trimmed shift, his thumbs teasing her nipples into tight peaks. A moan escaped her throat and she sagged on his lap.

"Touch them, Stephen. Suckle them." She gripped his shoulders, not caring if her command made her seem wanton. "I want to feel your mouth on me." When he did as she asked, a thrill speared her insides and desire coiled low in her belly.

"It is a crime these are kept hidden from view." He buried his face between her breasts. "Your body should be worshipped, adored by men." When he pulled away, he again palmed the mounds, lightly squeezing before sucking a nipple into his mouth.

Maggie moved a hand to the back of his neck, her fingers threading into his damp hair. She held him closer. "I don't want men, only you." He licked the hardened tip, tormented it with his tongue. The steady drum of the rain on the carriage top drowned her moan. She'd missed this intimacy. She pressed her body against his, and he responded by switching his attention to her other breast. Tingles played her spine. Need spiraled through her insides. She wanted more.

When his teeth grazed her nipple, she gasped, but when he blew warm air on her moist skin, she shivered at the coolness. How could a bit of air and wetness have the power to turn her into such a shameless woman? Her head lolled on one shoulder. "Don't stop." Perhaps she'd been alone too long without experiencing a man's touch. Maybe she craved the release coupling with Stephen would bring. Whatever force rode through her limbs, her every nerve ending, she knew she wanted this man—wanted him thoroughly and immediately.

"Stephen, please." Maggie fumbled with his cravat, but the intricate folds of the fabric confused her lust-fogged brain. She left off and attempted to work the buttons of his shirt. When she could only undo one due to her shaking fingers, she whimpered her frustration and moved to his waistcoat. Surely she could divest him of this piece of clothing! The buttons proved too much for her to accomplish, so instead, she gripped his shoulders and ground her hips into his, seeking harder contact.

Hot sensation ebbed from the tiny bundle of nerves at her center. "Oh." It wasn't enough.

"Tell me what you like, Maggie." Stephen trailed his lips beneath her jaw and peppered kisses down her throat. "What will it take to make you come undone?"

Her mouth went dry. "I..." How did she tell a man she'd met days ago that she wanted him to have wild, abandoned intercourse with her? It was one thing to think those naughty thoughts, but quite another to voice them aloud. "I want..."

"It's all right." He brushed his lips over hers. "At times, it's perfectly acceptable to allow the man the lead, especially when he knows exactly what you need."

"Do you?" She held his dark gaze. His sense of confidence, his consummate charm, gripped her deeper than a mere carnal connection could. What sort of man was he when he wasn't angling to get her into bed? Yet, sitting on his lap with her bosom exposed and her skirts bunched around her legs in a broken-down carriage where anyone could come upon them, she felt wicked, even decadent. The other thoughts would keep until the passion cleared.

"I believe I do."

A smiled curved her lips and she pressed her mouth to his ear. "I'm anxious to find out if what you've planned is indeed what I want."

"You won't be disappointed." Stephen fought through the yards of fabric covering her hips then a warm hand cupped a buttock while the other stroked the inside of one of her thighs. He shifted on the bench, spreading his legs, which naturally caused hers to open wider. "But you might be quite bothered. I want to see you fly."

Maggie bit her bottom lip. Her legs quivered from the new position. "Go on." When his hand remained stationary on her thigh, she quelled a sob of frustration. "For the love of God, please touch me."

"There is something quite satisfying about keeping a woman perched on the brink and waiting until she begs for more." He squeezed the hand at her bottom.

Shivers chased over her skin, and she didn't mind that he manipulated her pleadings as she'd done with him. "You know where I want you."

"I do." Finally, the hand at her thigh moved. He massaged her skin and left tingles in their wake. "I believe this is what you're after." His fingers moved higher, teased her curls and oh so slowly, inched upward to stroke her swollen folds.

"Oh, Stephen." Maggie's breathy moan betrayed the force of her need. She didn't care. Her whole world revolved on his hand at her most intimate of places. Through the layers of skirting, she pressed his hand against her. "Yes."

"I enjoy a woman who has no qualms about showing her enjoyment." He dropped a kiss on her mouth and slid his fingers over her sensitized flesh. "I love how you feel, so warm, so wet and welcoming." He stroked the length of her folds, swirled a finger around her center then returned upward. "So ready for sinning."

Her breath came in pants. She couldn't breathe; she couldn't concentrate on anything except the touch of his fingers and the heat he coaxed from her. Again, she guided his hand, wishing like mad he'd tease her sex, find that all-important spot she needed him to play with.

"Poor Maggie. I think you're in dire want of this." Stephen rubbed a forefinger over her nubbin and chuckled when she squirmed. "Ah, I thought so. Perhaps I'll linger here." He increased the friction on her button, flicking his finger over and around it. "So much feeling in such a tiny bit of the female anatomy."

"Mmm." She closed her eyes and moved her hips in time to his stroking. Pleasure spiraled tight in her core. Unbearable pressure coiled, ready, waiting to spring. Her breasts ached, mirroring the exquisite need he'd introduced into her body, and she brushed them against his chest. The rough textures from his evening clothes scraped over her taut nipples and added to the shaking torment her being had become. "Almost..."

"Show me how badly you want release." His finger moved ever faster, harder. With his other hand, he stroked her rear and pressed her closer.

Maggie bit her bottom lip. She rotated her hips, guiding his hand tighter on her sex. Needing added insurance to send her over the edge, she pinched a nipple, rolling it between her thumb and forefinger. Sharp pain-tipped bliss shot through her breasts and chased down to mingle between her thighs. "Please."

"I'm trying, love." He circled her swollen nub and took the nipple she wasn't ravaging into his mouth.

The sensation of his lips and teeth did the trick. The pooling tension broke, and she shattered. "Oh my!" Bliss swelled and crashed over her in one consuming wave. Heat tingled over her skin. It ebbed throughout her limbs and down to her fingertips and toes until her bones had the strength of jelly. She slumped against him and buried her face in the crook of his shoulder. His clean scent perfumed the air she sucked in as her pulse hammered from her exertions. "I have truly missed this."

His chuckle rang of smug, satisfied male as he withdrew his hands from beneath her skirts. "Next time, I wish to hear my name on your lips when you spend."

"Aren't you full of cheek?" She exhaled on a shuddering sigh and raised her head, seeking his gaze. He'd brought her to completion with as much ease as if he'd known exactly how she needed to be touched. Was that because he'd been in tune with her body and wished to please her, or had he gained such experience with a bevy of women, who'd found themselves in her same position at one time?

Why did it matter so much?

Maggie shook her head, hoping to clear her thoughts. "Even still, I think I'll keep you."

"I should hope so. This is only half of what I can impart. I'm not willing to give you up so soon." He held her head between his palms, and he kissed her so thoroughly her head spun. "If this damn carriage hadn't broken down, I would have—"

A sharp rap on the window interrupted his speech.

"Hell's bells." Frissons of anxiety invaded her lethargy. Maggie tugged at the bodice of her gown, hurriedly smoothing the satin and lace over her breasts that still ached for him. "What a time to be interrupted."

"You won't hear an argument from me."

"I knew help would come, obviously. I had hoped it wouldn't arrive quite so soon."

"How interesting your ire rises in conjunction with your frustrated urges." Stephen eased her off his lap and onto the bench beside him. Unfortunately, she crushed his top hat beneath her.

"Quickly, do up my buttons." She turned her back. Seconds later, the warmth of his fingers heated her exposed skin as he manipulated the fastenings. How regretful her clothing was going on instead of off. When his fingers whispered across her nape, she faced him, regardless of her twisted jumble of skirts. "What now?"

He passed a hand through his hair. "Go out to meet the lions I suppose." Another sharp rap on the window followed.

"Wait." She fumbled around on the floor and grabbed his discarded evening jacket. "You'll need this." When she held up the garment, he shoved his arms through and tugged it straight into some semblance of respectability. With an intense look, he swung open the carriage door. Glancing over his shoulder at her, he said, "Stay here until I can ascertain the disturbance. I'd rather you stayed safe and dry." Stephen jumped from the disabled vehicle and the door closed.

Maggie stared into the darkness, a silly smile tugging at her lips. She appreciated his concern for her well-being. It would seem he had other coveted qualities beyond his charm and skill in giving carnal pleasure.

The murmur of masculine voices blended with the rain. She stood as best she could in the tilting carriage and shook out her skirts. At least they covered her lower half now. Casting about for her missing gloves, she gave up the search after only finding one. Where had the blasted thing gone? Her foot bumped into her hat. Quickly sitting, she retrieved the headgear and put it on, securing it with the hat pin. She must look a mess, and in strong light under a sharp eye, anyone with half a brain would know her appearance wasn't solely due to a carriage mishap.

Her grin widened. *I don't care what the tabbies say. I enjoyed myself this evening.*

Yet her hunger for Stephen hadn't slacked. It circled through her body like a prowling beast. At the first opportunity, she'd get him alone, drag him to a secluded area if need be, and have her way with him. After that, she intended to have a heart-to-heart talk. He should know some of her history and she wanted to hear his, perhaps ascertain what else he wanted from life. Yes, she wanted the scandal, but maybe her need for him was too great for a fling. If so, what then?

The door opened once more, and Stephen stood peering in. "Your brother had his driver circle back. It would seem young Billy rode after Alfred's carriage instead of chancing a trip to your estate." He extended a hand. "Come. We can all ride to the squire's party, and make a fashionable entrance together."

"How lovely." No longer did she wish to spend the evening at the rout, making forced conversation with the local gentry or watching Amanda simper and blush at the young men. She stood and slipped her hand into his. "I hope this evening passes quickly as I have other plans."

"As do I." Stephen nodded. "On second thought, it's a dangerous leap to the ground. Please accept my assistance." He released her hand, moved his to either side of her waist and then lifted her out of the carriage. Alfred stood off to one side, a lit lantern swinging from an upraised hand. Billy, astride the horse, sat near the rear of the coach.

"Thank you." She gripped his shoulders as he held her far too close for a tad longer than necessary. His dark gaze bored into hers and was shadowed with emotions she couldn't identify in the flickering lantern light. Steady on her feet, she moved away and immediately regretted the loss of his body heat. "Ah, there is my missing glove. It must have fallen from the carriage when you exited." The errant glove lay muddied in a puddle, but neither she nor Stephen moved to retrieve it. They simply stared at each other while rain soaked his hair and tapped on her hat.

Alfred cleared his throat. "If I could advise getting out of the rain? I'd rather not become any wetter than necessary in this foul English weather."

"Yes, of course," Stephen murmured. He ushered her to the large coach and yanked open the door. "In you go, Lady Parker."

Maggie hitched up her skirts and climbed the steps, choosing to take a seat between Nanny Beatrice and Amanda.

The men entered shortly afterward and sat on the bench opposite, and the coach lurched into motion.

"Horrid weather tonight, huh, and rather cold?" Maggie wiped at the moisture on her face, hoping if anyone noticed her appearance or high color they'd attribute it to the stress of the carriage mishap. "I hope the delay hasn't diminished your excitement for this evening, Amanda." She refused to glance across at Stephen. She couldn't, not when her insides still roiled with leftover desire.

Her niece turned toward her, her eyes narrowed. "Just what happened back there, Aunt Margaret?"

"Whatever do you mean, child? A wheel broke upon hitting a hole in the road. As Mr. Tarkington and I waited for assistance, the axle went as well, leaving us cooling our heels in a crazy tilting carriage." She lifted an eyebrow. "Are you implying I arranged for vehicle trouble?"

"No, but I find it highly suspect, especially after your stint with the rabbit hole from yesterday. Really, Aunt Margaret, alone with Mr. Tarkington for all those minutes? What transpired between you?" Amanda crossed her arms beneath her bosom and pouted.

"Nothing that bears mentioning." Maggie refused to let the young woman intimidate her into a slip of the tongue. "Why, Amanda dear? Does my appearance resemble that of a woman who has been thoroughly molested or done anything remotely less than proper?" Her tone dared her niece to disagree. "Even I can only do so much with the rain."

A choking sound from Stephen shot into the quiet, but she ignored it—and him. She had to. If she looked his way, she'd want to throw herself into his arms and begin her seduction all over again, but dear Lord, she hoped his buttons were all in place since she'd destroyed his hat.

"Well, Mr. Tarkington *is* missing his hat," Amanda accused.

"Easily explained as it was crushed when he tried to ascertain the extent of damage to the undercarriage." Maggie couldn't believe how easily the lie tripped off her tongue.

Amanda huffed. "Then there are your missing gloves. How did they come to be off, Auntie? Not to mention your hat is decidedly crooked and you are quite flushed."

As her stomach knotted, Maggie searched for some explanation but came up lacking. "Challenging your elders is akin to a social gaffe, Amanda."

"I apologize." The younger woman spat out the words then turned her face to the window. "You and Mr. Tarkington look almost as lovely as you did when we left the house."

"Thank you for the compliment, Miss Manning," Stephen offered, to the apparent amusement of Alfred.

"It's unfortunate Mr. Tarkington's ensemble is incomplete. I was hoping to dance with him this evening and perhaps show him off to the local girls." Amanda still stared out the window.

"What difference does his appearance make? He's mostly intact." Maggie's ribs hurt from stifling her laughter.

Amanda turned her head and stared at her aunt. "He won't compliment me now."

"Such talk makes you appear shallow, Amanda." Maggie couldn't believe the gall of her niece. "Besides, I had thought you promised David Collins you'd accompany him around this evening as it is his welcome we're celebrating."

"He is but one male, Aunt Margaret. Shouldn't I acquaint myself with as many in Surrey as I can?"

Oh, bother. Maggie wished her brother Gregory was here. She would give him a tongue lashing or two on how he'd raised Amanda. "There is nothing worse than a fickle woman, Amanda. Pray see that you don't embarrass yourself or me this evening."

"Yes, Aunt. I cannot wait to be free of this coach to mingle with those of my own age."

"I do apologize, dear. I suppose we all cannot wait to return home so we might put our feet up in bed with a cup of tea." While both Alfred and Stephen snickered, Maggie risked a peek at Stephen. He gave a nearly imperceptible wink, and flutters cut loose in her belly. Having an affair was such fun! Imagine a lifetime of such hijinks and teasing. Except... well, an affair didn't mean a lifetime, did it?

Nanny Beatrice touched Maggie's arm. "Women who don't wear gloves have the best adventures. Consider yourself lucky."

Just what scandals had her nanny been involved in during her youth? "Mmmhmm." Maggie bit back a smile and relaxed into the seat. *I heartily agree.*

Chapter Seven

After the squire's rout, they'd returned to the Parker estate too late to make good on Stephen's promise of bedding Maggie. Though she had seemed alert and flushed after Amanda's apparent success, he suspected she was tired—the drooping of her smile and dull twinkle in her eye had proclaimed it. On the stairs, he'd whispered in her ear that perhaps relations should wait until the light of day. She'd bestowed upon him a look of such gratitude, and something bigger he couldn't figure out, that he felt he'd fly if he jumped off the roof. But she hadn't agreed to an assigned time or place.

What in creation did that mean?

Birdsong overhead broke into his thoughts. Stephen lifted his face to the noon day sunshine and gloried in the late spring warmth. After last night's rain and chill, the pleasant weather was exactly what he needed to reaffirm that being at the Parker estate was a good thing. Of course it was; any chance to spend time with Maggie was a good thing—a great thing. The time spent with her in the broken-down carriage had been too short, and he wanted more. He wanted to know the real Maggie, the woman behind the passion, to find out what else she wanted from her life—and whether she'd ever thought beyond the affair.

Would they play it out for a while and then tire of each other, going their separate ways after a time, perhaps meeting in London for a few events with a civil nod and a smile... and memories of desire forgotten?

His stomach clenched as he walked along the edge of an idyllic pond he'd found on the property. Before meeting Maggie, he had no plans of remarrying, and realized now that the lame idea of aligning himself with Amanda was decidedly ill-advised. He'd been adamant he had no use for the institution, and could never live up to his parents' example. Now, the thought of marriage entered his mind more and more, and it centered around Maggie. She'd be the type of woman who'd make marriage a permanent event. Would she consider an alliance for a lifetime—with him—and did he want to inquire?

It was too soon to tell. He knew next to nothing about her. After all, one dalliance in a carriage didn't lay enough foundation to build dreams upon.

Stephen's snort of laughter sounded out of place in the tranquil setting. Dreams. A lifetime with someone. Marriage. He must be daft if he was ruminating on the state of his heart. Love couldn't happen in a handful of days, and he wasn't handy in the romance department. Two failed marriages were a testament to that. One wife dead and the other one who hated him to the depths of her soul as evidenced by her behavior when they'd applied for the annulment. Not to mention his ego, more than his reputation, had taken the brunt of her vitriol. He'd had to testify that he was impotent and had lied about it in order to marry the minx to begin with.

Marriage was the crux of the problem. If he kept Maggie in a mistress capacity, everything would work out fine, except both his head and his heart vehemently protested such a decision, and besides, once she knew of his annulment, would she even want him? He'd rather Maggie remember him with fondness instead of ire.

He shoved a hand through his hair. What the hell was a man to do with such a conundrum? Stephen ducked beneath the overflowing bows of a weeping willow. A cluster of the trees hugged the edge of the pond, creating a botanical curtain of sorts and shelter from sight of the road some distance away. He leaned a shoulder against one of the tree trunks and crossed his arms over his chest. In the distance, the rooftop of Maggie's home barely peeked above the tree line. Black-and-white cows dotted the pasture lands nearby. A few geese floated on the far end of the pond, and the thick blanket of grass provided a vibrant green backdrop to the area. After breathing in a deep lungful of air, he let it ease out on a sigh. Sunlight filtered through the slightly swaying boughs. A man could get used to this view.

"Either you're thinking on a particularly lovely thought, or you've made a decision. You have the look of a man who might have done both."

Stephen startled at the sound of Maggie's voice. Heat curled through his body as it always did when she approached. He pushed away from the tree. She came up a slight rise and joined him under the tree branches. She stopped two feet in front of him, placing a basket near her feet as she did so. The canopy surrounded her and framed her with an organic green glow. "Perhaps it is both. Too early to say." He touched the brim of his beaver pelt hat. He could puzzle out his thoughts later. "Good afternoon, Maggie."

"Hello, Stephen." She made no move to close the distance between them. Neither did he. Once he took her into his arms, there would be no going back.

"I needed a place to think and came upon this spot. I rather like it." He focused his gaze on the swans as they plunged their long necks into the water and then raised them up again.

"The pond is a favorite spot of mine as well. Last summer, the parson caught me as he strolled the road. I was swimming naked." Her giggle wafted on the air and swirled around him before the levity slid from her expression. "It's a special place with much meaning for me." Her blue eyes took on a faraway look.

"How's that?" He caressed her with his gaze. Tendrils of brown hair, fallen from the knot at the back of her head, framed her face. Today, she wore no bonnet, and the sun made her tresses gleam a rich caramel color. He loved seeing it flowing free.

"I came here the day my husband died in order to grieve in private. He didn't care for outward displays." She smiled, but it didn't reach her eyes. "I played with my son here many times. He had a fondness for the waterfowl."

"I think all young boys do. I can't tell you how many times I ended up in lakes or creeks as a lad."

The smile wavered. "There's a family cemetery not far from here. That's where the baron is buried as well as my dear Jamie. When I come here, I feel close to my boy."

"You have my condolences." Would she tell him about her son? He wanted to understand more of what drove her. "What do you miss most about Jamie?" He glanced at her and his stomach bottomed out at the glimmer of tears in her eyes.

"Oh, that is hard to say. There are so many things." Maggie took a few steps toward him. Her rose-colored skirt brushed the ground. "The way he said 'ma'. The way his eyes lit up when something caught his interest. The sweet sound of his breathing when he slept." The tendons in her neck worked with a swallow. "I sometimes cannot believe it's been ten years since I lost him. He would have been a lovely young man I think"

"I'm sure he would have." Again, the swans caught his attention. So graceful, so unconcerned at the emotion roiling between the two humans beneath the willow. "It's been thirteen years since my first wife and only child died in childbirth." The need to unburden himself grew strong. "Neither of us was prepared when the contractions started. The babe—a girl—had been breech, and the complications were too much. By the time the doctor arrived, Jane had lost too much blood. Sarah was stillborn, most likely suffocated." His chest tightened and his heart squeezed with the sadness he would always carry. "Missing loved ones leaves marks on our souls," he rolled his shoulders as tension pooled there, "gives us experience and motivation to go on, I suppose."

"How long had you been married?" Maggie clasped her hands at her waist.

"Six months. I'd barely graduated university and been lucky enough to start in the import business at the lowest entry position. Not long after we'd been introduced, we, uh, were rather naughty one night following a ball and as fate had it, we were forced to marry. Her father saw to that." God, he'd been so irresponsible. Guilt lay heavy in his gut. "Perhaps it was my fault Jane died. If I hadn't pushed to have relations, hadn't pressed…"

"Oh, no, you can't think like that." Maggie closed the distance between them and slipped her arms around his middle. "Remember the happy times with her. You said yourself that life has given you experience. You couldn't have known what would happen, but because it did, you're a stronger, better man."

Stephen held her close, grateful for her presence. She hadn't censured him or condemned him on decisions he'd made while too young to know better. He tucked her head beneath his chin; she was the perfect height. "I often wonder what my life would have been like had they both lived."

"I know that thought well. I've spent many sleepless nights wondering and berating myself for ever letting Jamie learn to ride, but he enjoyed it so." Several minutes of silence went by as his pulse rushed in his ears and the heat from her body seeped into him. The crisp rasping of the willow's leaves worked to whisk away the leftover grief.

"Did he ride every day?" Stephen wished he could have seen them both on their daily outings, Maggie with a little boy who had her looks and daring. His heart squeezed.

"Oh, yes. He was so proud of his pony. I'd only turned my back for a few seconds, but Jamie, always a precocious thing, urged his mount into a run and tried to jump a small creek at the back of the property." A tiny hiccup interrupted her speech. "The pony, with more sense than my boy, stopped abruptly. Jamie flew over its back and struck his head on a boulder. He broke his delicate, little neck, and my life changed forever."

"*Shh*, it's all right." He rocked her back and forth, as if the motion would soothe her memories. He wished he could give her new memories to offset the old ones.

Finally, she rubbed her cheek against his chest. "However, if they had lived, I would have never had the opportunity to be the woman I am today or to meet you."

"This is true." He pressed a kiss into her hair and inhaled her lilac scent. Did she keep dried flowers with her clothes, bathe with it in her water, or wash with soap infused with its oils? He could easily envision her as a calming influence in his life, his voice of reason. Did she enjoy the mornings or was she a difficult riser? These were only a small number of things he wished to know about her. "What are you doing out here, Maggie? I would have thought your ball tonight occupied all your attention."

"It's been planned down to the last detail, and with Caruthers and Cook in charge of most things, I essentially have nothing to do except wait. In fact, Caruthers shooed me out from under foot, and I gladly went for Amanda is in a snit. I lectured her regarding her flirtatious behavior last night and how that might put her in an unfavorable light with the males. She, of course, refused to listen to wisdom, so let's hope the young men turn a blind eye, at least for as long as this ball."

"Your niece is willful. I imagine she'll be as unforgettable as her aunt." Amanda could in no way rival Maggie. The younger woman was volatile due to youth and not knowing what she wanted from the future; Maggie was eccentric in a charming way and knew exactly what she wanted.

"Look at you putting on the cheek." She pulled away in order to hold his gaze. In the sunlight, a smattering of freckles decorated the bridge of her nose.

"So you decided to take the air?"

"Not exactly. When I didn't find you in the house, I came outside to search the grounds for you."

"Why?" He knew why, but his ego needed to hear her say it. Their time together had led to this moment. "Tell me, Maggie." His cock pressed against his trousers. He wanted her—wanted to claim her as his—wanted, for one perfect moment, to be everything she needed.

"Don't be daft, Stephen. I want the same thing you do—to finish what we started in the carriage last night."

The desire that had simmered just below the surface during their somber sharing rushed into being once more. "Are you certain? The earlier conversation didn't suggest the appropriateness for passion."

"Those memories will always be with us. That doesn't mean we shouldn't live while remembering them."

He held her darkened gaze. With very little effort he could drown in those depths and die a happy man. "Where?"

"Why not here?" She gestured at their private sanctuary. "As I said, it's special to me. It would be even more so should we consummate our affair."

His heartbeat skittered. She considered relations with him special? "The ground might very well be damp from last night's rain." He imagined he felt the coolness of the earth contrasting with the warmth of her body. His member twitched with anticipation.

"That won't bother me." She pointed to a basket on the ground nearby. "I brought a quilt that will lend goodly protection."

A grin curved his lips. She'd anticipated him and come prepared. "The location is risky. Anyone can come upon us. Perhaps even the poor parson who caught you before."

Her shrug pulled her lace-trimmed bodice tight across her bosom. "When my husband was alive, I spent too many years living a half-life due to avoiding risk. Now I live for me, for the experience, for the fun, for the scandal, to feel everything and know I didn't waste a minute." One of her eyebrows inclined. "Will you be as brave?"

"I swear you will be my undoing." Stephen tugged her into his embrace. He started to lift her skirts. "But you are correct. One should spend life living instead of talking about it." He cupped her bare buttocks. Her skin was silky against his palms. He pressed his hips into hers.

"Then you and I will get along fine." She twined her hands behind his neck. "Shall we retrieve the blanket?"

"In a moment." Part of seduction was enjoying the anticipation. He squeezed her ass, her soft skin warming his palms. Would she be daring enough to let him take her from behind? "For a progressive-thinking woman, I would have thought you'd adopted drawers some of the ladies wear now." Moving one hand up the back of one of her thighs, he encouraged her leg upward, and she curled it around his hip. Her heat beckoned, but he aimed to tease first.

She curved a hand at his nape, pulling his head closer to hers. "I do when the weather requires it, but in this instance, I decided the less clothing, the better. Ease of access outweighs fashion."

"Intelligent as well as beautiful."

"I left off with the stays too. There should be no barriers to pleasure."

"I love your frame of mind." He claimed her lips in a gentle kiss at the same time he slipped a hand around the curve of her rear to caress her folds slick with arousal. When she clasped him tighter and bit his bottom lip, he swiped a finger over her flesh, rubbing back and forth. Goaded by her increased breathing, Stephen explored further then flicked her swollen button with his forefinger. "Show me how much you want me, Maggie. Let me hear it."

Her head tipped backward, revealing the slender line of her throat. Stephen licked the dip between her collarbones.

"Oh..."

Stephen grinned. "What was that?" Watching her embrace her femininity caused his cock to pulse. His member prodded the front of his trousers. The need to throw her on the ground and bury himself deep took hold, but he wanted her to spend first, harder than her release in the carriage.

"More." She straightened, her fingers digging into his shoulders. She sighed against his throat.

There was no woman quite like Maggie. He increased the pressure on her sex and swirled his finger around the nub, over it, back and forth. "How much do you want satisfaction, Maggie? I'm not convinced." Stephen tightened his grip around her with his free hand. "I'm afraid I won't be able to drive my cock into you unless you come undone."

"You are an evil man, Mr. Tarkington." Heavy panting followed her statement. She nipped the side of his neck.

"No, just determined to give you pleasure." Leaving off with his torture, he slid his fingers over her moist folds, stroking the flesh before returning to her swollen nubbin. On his next pass, Maggie's body shook. She raised her head and reared slightly back, her eyes rounded with surprise. Stephen circled the button again. She shuddered. A flush spread over her chest. "Stephen!" He held her close while her shivers lessened. She went pliant and her leg slid from its position on his hip.

"Excellent." His cock twitched. There was more to be done. "We should find that quilt now." He released her and regretted the loss of her heat against him.

"Right." Maggie shook out her skirts. "Our flirtation this week has been most trying." She moved with wobbly steps to the reed basket and withdrew a faded green-and-yellow quilt. As she unfurled the blanket, Stephen grabbed the ends and helped her spread the material over the springy moss and grass beneath the tree branches.

"Shall we?" He shrugged out of his coat and, uncaring if it wrinkled, tossed it to the far corner of the quilt.

She toed off her slippers and knelt on the blanket. Her hardened nipples were visible beneath her bodice. "Hurry."

"Patience, my dear." Her eagerness stoked his desire. "Removing clothes is much like unwrapping a gift. With you, I intend to enjoy every second."

She shook her head, her blue eyes shadowed with the same longing he felt. "My need for you is too great." She pulled at her dress, gathering handfuls of it in her struggle to tug it over her head. "Next time, I demand you come to my bedroom with preferably less clothes and do this properly." The cloud of clothing muffled her command.

His heart pounded so hard he feared he'd have an apoplexy. "Then you plan to continue the affair for some time?" Stephen removed his waistcoat and dropped it on top of the coat before applying himself to the task of undoing the neck cloth. He pulled it from its intricate design and then raced to undo the shirt buttons. Finally, the garment gaped open. The faint breeze ruffled his chest hair and added another level of awareness to the proceedings.

Maggie separated herself from the gown and sat clad only in her shift, so sheer it barely hid her charms. "I'm keen on considering it." She raked her gaze over his torso as slowly as if she caressed him with her hands. "You're quite a fine specimen."

Heat swirled over his skin. He yanked off the shirt and neck cloth and tossed them away. The hunger in her eyes sent a throb of urgency along his shaft. It would take a fair amount of willpower to keep from spilling his seed too early, and he wanted their first coupling to be memorable.

"Stephen, please finish undressing. The teasing you gave me did little to cool my ardor." She tugged on one of his hands and he fell to his knees on the blanket. "Nevermind. I'll help you out of the last of it."

A rush of anticipation tingled through his body, and he gladly gave himself over into her care.

Maggie pressed a kiss to the cleft in Stephen's chin. She shoved at his shoulders, laughing when he toppled onto his back. She adored how masculine he looked with the butterfly-shaped mat of black hair spreading over his chest and loved how solid he felt beneath her hands as she traced the dark ribbon down over his abdomen to his waistband. What would that hair feel like scraping against her nipples? "Let's hope your boots don't require Alfred's valet." As she grabbed his left foot, she caught his eye. "Do you want to say something?" A hearty tug separated the boot from his foot. She tossed it to one side then reached for the other.

"I appreciate a woman who knows what—or who—she wants."

"Where you're concerned, I know exactly that." She pulled off the second boot and threw it to the side. "Now the trousers." The thought of putting her mouth on him again sent a throb of desire into her core. "Would you like me to give you an abbreviated rendition of what I did to you in the carriage?"

"That won't be necessary. I'm more than ready." He unfastened the buttons then shoved his trousers and short pants down. His erect cock sprang free. It curved toward his belly from a nest of dark curls. "I've wanted you since the dressing down you gave me in the rose arbor."

Her mouth watered. She'd let him have his way today, but their next coupling would involve her pleasuring him orally. Already she anticipated the salty tang of his seed on her tongue. Since that one, brief time with her husband, she'd craved just that. Thank goodness Stephen seemed a man who'd let her have her way. "My censure wasn't fierce enough since that interlude ended only with your hand in my bodice." A tug separated his legs from the clothing, and finally he was free—and hers. "You're so wonderfully large." Maggie leaned into him and cupped his length and sac. When he groaned, she squeezed with care and his member jerked against her palm. "I need you, Stephen." Though mutual flirtation was great fun, nothing would compare to feeling him in her body.

He batted her hands away from his person. "As soon as I remove your shift, my dear. It's only right to see you tit for tat." After a series of maneuvering, he pulled the garment from her body. It joined the litter of clothing on the blanket. "You are beauty personified. I scarcely know what to admire first."

"I appreciate the compliment, but I am wanton and needy." Maggie refused to waste more time on conversation. She lay on the quilt and beckoned for him to follow. "No flattery. The dance we've done over the last few days has seemed an eternity."

"In that, you have my agreement." He spread her legs with a hand and shifted over her body to settle between the cradle of her bent knees. "However, I must warn you, this affair could possibly result in you being with child."

"Oh bother, Stephen." He wanted to talk about this now, when she was hovering so close to the edge of glory? She huffed and the expiration of breath ruffled his hair. "I'm too old to have any more children. There is no need for concern."

"Very well, but if time shows otherwise, I give you my word I'll take care of you and the child." Honesty blazed in his expression. "I've learned well from my past mistakes."

Tears crowded the back of her throat. "You consider relations between us a mistake?"

"God, no." He claimed her lips in a kiss that left no more doubts. When he allowed her breath, he said, "This is the beginning of a mutual partnership wherein we'll both find satisfaction and joy." His gaze flicked to her breasts. "Yes or no in continuing, Maggie. I cannot last either way."

She smiled. How adorable he was when his need showed, but the fact he'd meet his obligations touched her heart. "Please continue. We've gotten rather off topic."

He dipped his head and caught one pebbled nipple in his mouth.

Maggie slid her arms around his shoulders while wriggling her hips. The tip of his cock kissed her opening. A moan escaped her throat, intensifying when he worried the nipple with his tongue. Delicious shivers circled through her lower belly. For days she'd thought of nothing except his moment. Now it was here and every bit as glorious as she'd imagined. "Stephen." She moved a hand to his nape and threaded her fingers through the soft hair there.

He wouldn't be rushed, no matter that she tilted her hips to encourage that first thrust. Instead, Stephen showed his appreciation to her neglected breast while he slid a hand down her side and gripped her buttock.

"Do not draw this out." She wriggled her hips and gasped as Stephen entered her in one smooth stroke. Maggie lost all track of her thoughts. He withdrew only to slide back in with a gentle rhythm that sent tiny shockwaves into her core with each pass. On her next sigh, he raised his head. She looked into his face and held his gaze. Emotions shadowed his beautiful gray eyes. What did he think about?

Stephen paused. He grinned but said nothing, only encouraged her arms over her head while he plundered her breasts with teeth, tongue and lips, laving them with a firm pressure that set tremors dancing over her skin. When he was done, he took them in hand and held them, pushed them together and devoured the nipples as if he'd never seen a naked woman before.

The contrast between the slow lovemaking and the frantic play at her bosom had Maggie's mind spinning. She gripped his upper arms. She whispered his name, trying not to drown in the sensations he'd invoked in her body. Stephen merely grinned again. He gave her a wink then levered upward and rested his hands beside her. He leaned over her body and slammed into her passage with short, forceful strokes.

The spiraling pressure sailed higher and tighter. Each time his cock brushed her sex, ripples of desire rolled through her and added to the exquisite ache building deep in her core. Just as she became accustomed to the new tactics, Stephen paused again and resumed his conquest of her breasts. The thrusting cycle started over with the slow, gentle rhythm.

Gooseflesh raced along her skin the closer to release she came. Every look, every touch, every change in penetration, every shared breath she took with him bonded her to him in ways she'd never encountered. Not even with her late husband had she felt so fulfilled on all levels.

"More." Maggie thought she might burst. Her body fairly hummed.

"I can't last." Stephen dug his fingers into her hips and lifted her lower half off the blanket as his hips hammered harder, faster. The slap of his flesh against hers rang in her ears in time to her ragged breathing. "Maggie..."

She didn't hear the rest. At his next thrust, she shattered. White light burst behind her eyelids. Her body exploded into a mixture of wild, heated sensations. His cock pulsed within her and her passage responded in kind, convulsing and squeezing around his shaft. Bliss rippled up from her core, the warmth of his seed shot deep, while tremors continued through her body and tingled into her breasts before ebbing away leaving her sated and tired.

"Well, you certainly didn't exaggerate your skill." She slumped onto the blanket the same time Stephen collapsed beside her. Maggie smiled when he wrapped his arms around her and urged her backside flush with his front.

"It was acceptable. I'll give you that." But the smug satisfaction in his voice was unmistakable as was his ragged breathing in her ear.

The feeling of drowsiness persisted, and she indulged the pleasant floating bliss. "It was more than that." She covered his arms with hers. "How soon can I experience it again?" Oh, how she wanted to have him in her bed, in her arms, more than once. Some of her joy faded in the face of the ever-present questions. Would she be enough to keep him with her for far longer or would he grow bored and seek his pleasure elsewhere?

Chapter Eight

Maggie maneuvered onto her back. A delicious lethargy infused her limbs and left them heavy and pleasantly warm. She used one of Stephen's arms as a pillow and peered through the gently swaying willow boughs. Wispy white clouds trailed through the light blue sky and flirted across the sun. She cared not one whit about her naked state.

After much teasing and torment, her affair had irrevocably started. She and Stephen had finally embarked upon the physical aspect of their relationship. The results of the coupling had been frantic and had relieved a certain need, emptiness prowled her chest. A yearning for a deep connection glimmered, a hunger for something... more.

Something she could hold onto once the affair concluded, because it would have to, wouldn't it? *We cannot continue to thumb our noses at society and sin to our hearts content without resuming our normal lives.* How silly to think a man like Stephen would want to be fettered. Did she? For eight years she'd done as she'd pleased without needing to curb her lifestyle due to a man's dictates. Would she give all that up if Stephen was willing?

She bit her bottom lip. Too many questions and all for a simple affair that wasn't as simple as she'd first thought. "Stephen?"

"Yes?"

"Would you have married your first wife had you not gotten caught?" Perhaps starting in his history would give her more insight into his character. Charming could only go so far, but if a man's mettle wasn't based in strong stuff, he wasn't worth her time. "Were you fond of her?"

Stephen's sigh seemed to come from the ages. "I was, in a way. Of course, Jane and I had indulged in the carnal side early, before we'd really known about each other." He stroked a hand down one of her arms. "In the six months we were married, I wasn't home all that much as business held my attention."

Did that mean he hated being leg-shackled to the woman, or did he think of it as a duty and sought his pleasures at clubs in London? "Was it drudgery to come home to at the end of the day?"

"Quite the contrary." He rolled onto his side, dislodging her from his arm, propped his elbow on the ground and rested his head on his hand. "I enjoyed coming home to someone. Jane had no idea how to run a household, but she tried her best." A smile lifted the corners of his lips. "More often than not she, her abigail and the cook sat gossiping in the kitchen while nothing got done."

"Managing staff has a learning curve." She mirrored his state of recline. "Did you love her? Were you devastated when she died?" Did he feel deeply over things or was he merely a shallow man intent on warming beds and following his own desires?

"No. I felt the fondness of a friend for Jane." His eyes grew hooded, his expression guarded. "I did right by her, but to be honest, I was relieved when she passed—not because she had died, mind you, but that I wouldn't have the responsibility I'd never planned on."

Maggie's stomach clenched. It would seem he cared for no one except himself. Disappointment choked her. She quelled the tears tickling the back of her throat. "I see." She sat up and scooted to the edge of the blanket. As quickly as she could, she struggled into her abandoned clothing, wanting to shield her body from his eyes. "How nice to go through life treating people as if they don't matter."

"Now, Maggie, don't fly into the boughs on a misunderstanding."

"I'm not. I'm simply expressing my distaste for what you've done." The one time she allowed herself the freedom of an affair, she found her reasoning wrong.

"Will you judge me on the sins of my past after all?" He moved closer but didn't touch her.

"I'm not certain." When he slid a hand down her arm, she moaned. It would seem one fleeting caress by him had the power to dissolve her ire. Perhaps it wasn't fair to judge him based on one incident. She wouldn't want him to do the same with her. "I apologize." She didn't protest when he nudged her onto her back, his face hovering above hers, the hard wall of his body pressing into her softer curves.

"At least I didn't lie to you. I was young, and eager to start my life. Back then, I didn't understand the consequences of my actions."

She peered into his gray eyes, so much like storm-tossed seas, before glancing away. "I suppose once you were free, you were a gad-about, chasing the ladies, acting as any other gentleman with some coin and charisma behind him." Annoyed with both him and herself for her line of reasoning, she recaptured his gaze. "How many mistresses have you had?"

"You never cease to surprise me with your forward conversation. It's quite a refreshing change." Stephen chuckled and shifted over her. He insinuated a knee between her thighs and, through her skirts, rubbed against her most intimate of places.

A host of tingles erupted through her core. Maggie stifled a moan. "How many?" Why did she care how many women he'd been with? She had no right to him. She'd told him she wanted an affair only.

"Five, my dear, and one of them is you. Another was my second wife."

That left three other women who'd shared his life over the years. How long did those ladies last, and was he still keeping one in London, the woman he'd go back to when he left her? "Right, your second wife." Her stomach knotted. "But you're not married?"

"No, you silly goose." When she attempted to squirm from under him, he planted his hands on either side of her head and pressed his body tighter into hers. The musky scent of lovemaking clung to him and rekindled her hunger. "I may be considered a rogue in some circles, but I'd never conduct an affair while still wedded. In this, I pride myself on being better than some of the aristocracy."

She refused to acknowledge the relief that shuddered through her. Instead, she brushed at a lock of hair that had fallen over his forehead. He had the softest hair she'd ever felt on a man. "I assume she died?"

"Far from it."

"Perhaps you should explain." *And set my mind at ease.*

"I met Rosa while on a business trip to Barcelona. She worked in a club, and I was well into my cups one night." Stephen placed a kiss on her temple. The scarce stubble on his chin scraped her cheek and brought awareness with it. "It'd been a few years since Jane died, I was away from home and lonely. Rosa was there, willing and very persuasive. Our coming together burned hot, and I had proposed by the time I concluded my business, stupidly thinking what I felt was love."

"It wasn't?" She enjoyed feeling the length of his body on hers, loved the clean, earthy scent of him. Being so close to him played havoc with her common sense. She wanted to blurt out everything that tormented her. Yet she fought the urge.

"No. It was merely lust, but it was different from what I'd experienced with Jane. How would I have known it had no substance? Rosa and I were married in a tiny church the next month. The union lasted a grand total of five months and we fought like cats and dogs the whole time. Outside of the bedroom, we had nothing in common."

"Oh." Would that happen to her and Stephen? Did they share interests outside each other?

"Her Spanish blood didn't mesh well with my English sensibilities and goals. The process of gaining an annulment—for she could convince a dog he needed fleas with her lies—took longer than the actual marriage. Plus, she cited religious differences among other things, and in the Spanish courts, that holds more sway than what actually happened, but by then she'd thrown all my clothes into the street, moved out and gone back to Barcelona."

"My goodness. I'd say you really made an impression on her."

"Apparently, I lack the skills to ascertain what it takes to make a woman happy for a lifetime." He dipped his head and touched his lips to hers for a brief kiss. When he sought her gaze again, some of the sadness had faded. "Are there any other questions? I'd like to set your mind at ease." His warm breath feathered across her cheek. "I don't want our time together spoiled by ghosts of the past."

Her heart stuttered. "What of your mistresses?"

"What of them?" Stephen rolled over and took her with him. She reclined awkwardly across his naked body. "Over the years I've had female company. I'm a man, not a monk." He winked. "I can tell you none of them have graced my bed for many months now."

"I see." Maggie straddled him and braced her palms on his shoulders. He was lean and solid muscle between her thighs. What would it feel like to take her pleasure while astride him? A swift contraction rocked her core, and she gasped. How was it possible she wanted him again so soon? She shoved the thought to the back of her mind. He couldn't be allowed to distract her with his body and overt masculinity. "Do you think you'll marry again?" Yes, she'd asked him that a few days ago, but she held out a tiny hope he might have changed his mind.

If he did, then maybe she might also.

"That depends on a great many things, none of which I wish to discuss at this moment." He smoothed his palms up her legs and under her skirts. "What of you, Maggie? Will you marry again if the circumstances are right?"

She swallowed around the lump in her throat. Her fingers drifted through the hair on his chest. The intense look in his eyes stole her breath. Did he wish to know for general purposes or did something else prompt his question? "I... I'm not sure." For the first time in many years, she'd become nonplussed by a man. She'd wanted the affair. Now that it was hers, did wanting more mean marriage, and if it did, how would they work it—if at all?

Stephen chuckled and buried his nose in Maggie's hair. He grinned at her as she straddled him. Oh, how he loved catching her off guard. When she wasn't always confident and in control, vulnerability stole into her expression and darkened her gorgeous eyes to sapphire. In those moments, he wanted nothing more than to wrap his arms around her and protect her from anyone who meant her harm.

"Did your marriage sour you for the wedded state?" He stroked the outside of her thighs and moved his hands upward to play over the soft skin of her hips beneath the skirts.

"No, but it did teach me a thing or two." She straightened. The delectable curve of her bottom and the silk dress brushed his half-erect cock. Desire roared through his body. *Botheration*, he wanted her again, and soon. "Robert and I met through my father and his Navy cronies when I was a girl of seventeen. It seemed my father had friends in every Navy throughout the world. Robert had come into the barony by accident, you see. He was a third son. His brothers died in various military ventures courtesy of the Napoleonic Wars, with special exceptions and all that. The brothers had no children—one being impotent and the other never quite getting around to reproducing."

"And?" For such a progressive woman, she appeared awfully reticent to share.

"We met just as Robert decided to retire from service. He was nearly twenty years my senior. Father signed off on him as a suitor, and before I knew it, I was courted and married with military precision." Maggie shrugged. Though she stared at him, Stephen suspected she looked through him at the past. "We came to Surrey and settled down. My husband was… frugal, and beyond that, the country air didn't agree with him. He was always sickly and prone to every sneeze, sniffle, and lung ailment around."

"You were consigned to care for him while still in your youth." His chest welled with sympathy. "No wonder you choose to chase after scandal. It's the fun you were denied."

A faint smile touched her mouth. "Perhaps. Five years later, Jamie was born. I thought I'd explode with love and happiness." All too soon a frown stole away her previous joy. Tears misted her eyes. "Oh, I lived in the years he was alive. I had the excuse to be silly and ramble over the grounds whenever I wanted, laugh at the dragons' frowns, and play until my heart wanted to burst with the joy of it."

Stephen drew abstract designs on her skin. "Again, you have my condolences."

She waved away his words. "When I lost Jamie, I turned to Robert for guidance, healing, or just companionship, but he battled pneumonia at that time and anyhow, detested outward displays of emotion of any kind." Her throat worked with a swallow. "Robert died two years later following lingering complications from the disease. I was alone and free for the first time in my life."

"You enjoyed it." He pictured her in his mind's eye, a young woman of twenty-four, with a title and fortune, and all the time in the world to do what she pleased.

"Yes. I really did." Her smile wavered, but she didn't elaborate.

He withdrew his hands from beneath her skirts and then captured one of hers, tugging her flush atop top of him. "So I have my answer. You enjoy your life too much to toss it away on the gilded prison of marriage." His stomach clenched. But then, he hadn't expected anything less, had he, and he couldn't fault her for the choice.

"Circumstances change." She placed a kiss on his chin. "Right now, I don't want to think of the future." Another kiss followed beneath his jaw. She nibbled at a particularly sensitive spot under his ear that fired his blood. "I want to stay here until teatime, with you. I adore having you all to myself, especially naked as you are."

"I wholeheartedly agree with that plan." He rolled onto his side and held her close. He wanted more moments like this, when the outside world stayed at bay, and nothing required immediate attention. For this moment, Maggie was exclusively his—and he rather liked that thought. "At your ball tonight, I dare you to do something scandalous, something that will bring the sparkle back into your eyes."

Her laugh reverberated in his chest and tickled his ear. "I hope you're serious because I just might. I have nothing to lose."

As a tendril of her hair whispered across his cheek, Stephen sighed. *No, but I might.*

Later that night, Stephen stood in the foyer in the midst of a crush of people. Low murmurs chased through the crowd; excitement fairly crackled around him. Amanda's success in Surrey would be assured if the amount of attendees was any indication. Many in the crowd were young people Amanda's age, but there were others he assumed were Maggie's contemporaries as well as older folks, no doubt the local tabbies and society rule enforcers. He tugged at his gloves to ensure they were on as tight as they could go. Thank God they covered his sweaty palms.

Where is she? He darted a glance to the curving staircase. As of yet, no one appeared on the landing, but it wasn't Amanda he strained to see. Ever since he'd parted ways with Maggie around teatime, she'd been uppermost in his mind. Every beat of his heart whispered her name; every rush of his blood through his veins urged him to give into his thoughts and beg her to be his for more than an affair.

Common sense kept a tight grip on fancy. She'd given him no reason to think she'd welcome a suit from him. In a roundabout way, neither had he with her.

He inserted a forefinger between his neck and cravat. *Damn cloth is too tight.* He tugged. *Too many people here.* Candles flickered in sconces and in a great chandelier overhead. Sweat trickled down his spine. *Will no one open a window?* A hush rushed through the crowd and every head turned toward the landing. Stephen looked as well. His breath stalled in his chest, while heat consumed his body.

Maggie.

She stood next to Amanda, both of them dressed to the nines, but he could only concentrate on Maggie—*his* Maggie.

Dressed in lavender silk, she glowed under the candlelight. Crystal beadwork lined the square neckline of the gown and rimmed the capped sleeves. It sparkled on the skirt as she moved to the railing. White elbow-length gloves encased her shapely arms and a white feathered fan dangled from one hand. He couldn't wait to remove those gloves. A single strand of pearls graced her slim neck and drew his hungry gaze to her bosom. His throat closed. His member twitched. How he wanted to taste her satiny skin again, but he forced his gaze higher. Her blue eyes sparkled with pride and pleasure as she raised her free hand for silence.

A smile curved her kissable mouth. A circlet of sparkling amethysts and pearls lay threaded through her loose, upswept hair. Curling tendrils of the chestnut strands danced along her forehead and clung to her neck. "Thank you all for coming this evening. I'm as excited to introduce my dear niece, Miss Amanda Manning, into Cranleigh society tonight."

As if obligated, Stephen slid a glance to Amanda. She stood to Maggie's left. No less richly dressed than her aunt, Amanda seemed overblown somehow, as if she tried too hard and was ultimately eclipsed by Maggie's inherent grace and experience, but she appeared like an angel. Her blonde hair gleamed in the soft light, while her white gown shot with gold completed the ethereal image. She watched the crowd. When her gaze alighted on him, she narrowed her eyes and her rosebud mouth tightened.

Stephen's stomach knotted. He knew that look, and it meant impending doom. *What did the wench plan?* He peered around the gathering. The squire's son stood off to one side. Confusion warred with infatuation in his expression. *Something is afoot.* There was no time to dwell as Maggie began her speech.

"Since the age of seventeen, I've been a transplant to England, and Surrey in particular. I have a fond spot in my heart for my adopted country. Though my dreams of motherhood were thwarted by fate, I'm pleased for the opportunity to launch my niece into local society and then take her to London and watch her begin her adult life. She's as dear to my heart as my own offspring."

The assemblage politely clapped. Maggie's grin rivaled the candlelight. "Maybe now would be a good time for Amanda to say a few words then we'll open the ball with dancing. My brother Alfred will lead her out." She turned toward her niece. "Amanda, welcome to Cranleigh."

The young woman nodded, her gaze again sweeping the crowd. "Thank you, Aunt Margaret." A waver crept into her voice, and she cleared her throat. "As much as I appreciate this party tonight, I'm afraid I cannot start my adult life with a clear conscience." She paused, just enough to gain attention. "I'm living a horrible lie."

A ripple of curiosity caught the crowd like wildfire. They surged forward, every one of the guests straining. Nothing brought an event together like tasting scandal in the wind.

"Whatever do you mean, Amanda?" A frown marred the perfection of Maggie's expression.

Stephen's stomach dropped while cold dread spread through him. *This cannot be good.*

"When I came to your estate, Aunt Margaret, I had my heart set on a certain gentleman, but you stole him away from me. You told me I couldn't have him then you went after him yourself!" She added insult to injury by stamping her foot.

"What do you mean?" Maggie, with her smile still valiantly in place, affected an air of confidence, but Stephen saw the cracks in her armor—the shaking hand resting on the railing, the way she worried her bottom lip, her rapid intake of breath.

Stiff upper lip, my girl.

"What do you *think* I mean?" Amanda took a step backward, putting space between them. "Earlier today, David, I mean Mr. Collins, and I were walking the property. We saw you and Mr. Tarkington in a compromising position."

Maggie blanched. "I... I beg your pardon?" She swallowed. A blush stained her cheeks. "I rather think this isn't the venue to discuss such things."

Botheration. Stephen pushed his way through the crowd as discreetly as he could. He never took his focus from Amanda, who wore a tiny, satisfied smile, much like a cat who's just eaten the prized canary. *The little bitch is enjoying herself trying to destroy Maggie. Doesn't the chit realize without her aunt's backing, she'll have no Come Out?* His chest tightened, but he couldn't very well rush up the stairs and either carry away the jealous girl or shield Maggie.

"Oh, I think it is." Amanda patted her coif with a gloved hand. "You know *exactly* what I mean. I saw you. You and Mr. Tarkington were locked in an embrace. Your skirts were at your waist, your legs were exposed, and you were sitting *on top of him* doing God only knows what. Plus, he was *naked*!" She nodded, judgment, censure and triumph emanating from her as she peeked at the crowd.

Of course the gathering, ever ready for gossip, came up to scratch with several outcries and gasps of outrage.

"I... I'm not quite sure how to answer you." But her face had paled.

Stephen, buffeted by agitated movement, finally gained the edge of the throng. He stared at the landing as if his life depended on it, his concern only for Maggie. She gripped the railing, her face reflecting shock, her eyes huge, her jaw slightly slack. His heart lurched. He had to go to her, whisk her away, protect her from what would undoubtedly be a terrible surge of vitriol, yet a sick fascination kept him immobile.

"Well, Aunt Margaret, since all you do is preach to me about the ethics of courting, you need to face the consequences." Amanda clasped her hands in front of her, the picture of perfection and innocence. "Mr. Tarkington isn't yours, especially..." She paused and sought out his gaze, hers flat and cold. By the time she looked out over the crowd, she'd managed to bring a sparkling of tears to her eyes. "Especially since he compromised *me* in the coach while we traveled down here from London." A hiccup interrupted her revelation. "He should be mine."

Genuine shock reverberated through the crowd and echoed deep in his chest.

Damn and blast! Stephen's feet felt rooted to the floor. He couldn't move, could hardly breathe, but hundreds of pairs of eyes bored into him. Heat crept up the back of his neck, his ears and then into his cheeks.

Both he and Maggie exclaimed at the same time, "What?"

Chapter Nine

Black spots danced before Maggie's vision. "My God, Amanda, are you daft?" She closed her eyes and shook her head regardless of the low murmurs of outrage in the foyer below. *This cannot be happening.* Her stomach churned. Bile climbed into her throat. Her pulse rang in her ears. Would she end the night retching on the landing, or perhaps succumbing to a faint? No. She'd face the trouble head on like the baron and her father before him had taught her. As she straightened her spine, she opened her eyes. What would her father say? Meet one problem at a time and fight through the mess until it unraveled.

Heat enveloped her body while embarrassment sank into her consciousness. She drew in a deep breath and then blew it out. What conundrum should she focus on first—that her impressionable young niece witnessed her indiscretion with Stephen, that he'd potentially defiled that same niece before he'd met her, or that Amanda was so gauche she'd brought the whole scandal to the attention of Cranleigh society? Above all, she squelched the urge to look for Stephen. She couldn't. It was too dangerous, for if she saw him, her worst fears might be realized in his eyes. If that happened, she wanted it to be in private, not on a public stage.

As much as she'd love to wipe at the perspiration trickling over one temple, Maggie refrained. She would be the paragon of common sense in this little world gone mad. "Amanda," she kept her voice low and steady, "perhaps you should explain to me why you and young Mr. Collins were wandering the property, alone and without an escort. Where was Nanny Beatrice, or even your uncle?" She refused to dwell on just how much of her time with Stephen Amanda saw. If fate was kind, she hadn't witnessed the actual act itself. Yet, Stephen hadn't dressed until much later.

Oh, dear Lord.

"I... it didn't occur to me to ask." Amanda took another step backward. The curved railing on the landing halted her retreat. "David wished for a walk, and I agreed."

"Ah, I see." Movement down below caught Maggie's attention. She peered at the disturbance and bit the inside of her cheek to keep from laughing. David Collins had turned and run from the room, the tails of his coat streaming behind him. "It would seem your partner in crime has deserted you. Smart lad." She glanced at her niece. "Perhaps you should explain. I, as well as all your guests, am waiting."

"Fine." Amanda licked her lips. She cast her eyes downward, but when she glanced at Maggie, her gaze was still surly. "It's not fair that I've barely Come Out, while you've been wasting away around here for years, and the moment I bring home a gentleman you steal him from me."

Maggie nearly laughed at the girl's abject jealousy and blatant immaturity, but she quelled the urge. It would only make her seem petty, but she would take the chit to task later. "Mr. Tarkington, might I remind you, was never yours.

Commitments were not given. You forgot he existed, in fact, so great was your enthusiasm for gowns and your Season, not to mention your waffling interest in Mr. Collins or anyone else that happened to glance your way."

"I..."

"And I most certainly didn't steal Mr. Tarkington from you." Maggie continued on, choosing to ignore her niece's stammering. "He, as well as I, have free will and made decisions accordingly." She broke her own promise then, and peeked down. Her gaze collided with Stephen's.

Her breath stalled. He looked as sick as she felt, his gray eyes dark and shadowed, his face pale. *Poor man.* Butterflies took flight in her stomach, but couldn't quite chase away the dread that had built since Amanda's announcement. She didn't regret her time with Stephen. The start to her affair had been everything she'd hope for, and she wasn't willing to give him up on the grounds of her niece's tantrum—unless he'd well and truly molested Amanda. If that were the case, she'd put a knee into his willy herself.

Realizing the assemblage grew restless, Maggie smiled at the lot of them. The neighbors already knew she was eccentric, so making commands wouldn't harm her much more. As she closed the distance between her and Amanda, she grabbed the young woman's upper arm. "We can continue to air the family's dirty laundry in public and destroy your chances with all gentlemen, or we can discuss this in private."

Amanda tossed her head and attempted to pull away. "You are afraid of owning up to your indiscretion, Aunt Margaret."

"No, I am not." Maggie tightened her grip. "I haven't been afraid of anything since Jamie died. If I make mistakes, I accept the consequences." It was time to take the matter firmly in hand. She put her mouth to Amanda's ear. "It's in poor taste to start rumors, my girl. If I find out you're lying about Mr. Tarkington, I'll ship you back to America on the first boat. And I'll have plenty of stories to tell your father and grandfather about your behavior here."

"But..."

Conscious of all eyes on them, Maggie smiled as if it were all a great lark. "You'll find yourself in much more trouble once the men of the family get wind of your antics. More trouble than you're trying to cause here."

Whatever Maggie expected her niece to do, crying wasn't it. Big, fat tears rolled down Amanda's cheeks. "It's not fair, Aunt Margaret! No matter how many hints I dropped for Mr. Tarkington, he never touched me outside of lending me his arm, not even to give me a peck on the cheek. As soon as he met you, he acted enchanted, as if he'd never seen a woman before."

"I beg your pardon?" She loosened her grip on Amanda's arm as shock ricocheted through her chest.

Amanda rubbed at her tears, which further reddened her cheeks and nose. "You had your chance. Now you're on the shelf and dried up. Why won't a gentleman look at me the way Mr. Tarkington does you?"

"You're young. Give it some time. Also, for future reference, life isn't fair." She released Amanda's arm and turned toward the gathering. Her chest heaved as she tried to regulate her breathing. Stephen *hadn't* violated Amanda? The girl had fabricated the whole story? Maggie didn't know whether to laugh or cry, but her throat was tight with tears. Was it true

Stephen looked at her as if she'd enchanted him? Emotions roiled within her breast, and she had no time to analyze them, not in front of the assemblage.

Why hadn't she noticed Stephen's behavior?

She sought him out down below, but the crowd had shifted, hiding him from view. Regardless of the mess she'd become, the aftermath had to be dealt with. "Friends, may I have your attention?"

All eyes locked onto her. A wave of sickening heat rolled over her. *Dear Lord, I need some air.* "I believe my niece can benefit from some lemonade and perhaps a cake." She sent a pointed glare Amanda's way.

"You have no feelings, Aunt Margaret. I cannot believe you all but told them to look at me!" The girl sobbed into a handkerchief she pulled from her reticule and hurried down the stairs to the ground floor. Guests scattered to make way. A few of her contemporaries trailed after her.

Ah, the maudlin theatrics of the young. A smile twitched Maggie's lips. The girl would need to learn that words had consequences. "While she's availing herself of refreshments, please feel free to indulge yourselves. There are cards in one of the drawing rooms for the gentleman as well as a musical string performance in the front parlor, plus many other entertainments." Maggie snapped open her fan and swept air onto her overheated face. Fat lot of good the silly feathers did her. "Once Amanda has regained her customary sweet composure, she and her uncle will open the dancing. Dinner will be served near midnight."

The dismissal had barely faded into the low buzz of conversation of the guests when one of the matriarchs of Surrey came forward through the crowd. She and her husband hailed from outside Farnham with her husband holding a barony and lands much like Maggie's. The woman's one claim to fame was her daughter—who had been dragged to the wedding altar no less than four times and ran away from each. "A moment of your time, if you please Lady Parker. I'm afraid this latest scandal is the last straw for those of us living respectable lives."

Maggie stifled a sigh. *Oh, bother.* She edged toward the staircase and descended the first two steps. "Lady Underhill, whatever do you mean?" It was best to play the fool before the old woman. Early in her marriage, she'd attempted to antagonize the lady, and it had ended in half the county being divided in their allegiance.

The pudgy woman's nose went high into the air, her double chin quivering. "This latest escapade clearly shows you are not a fit sponsor for Amanda, let alone a fair representative for the barony. I think it best you remove yourself to London where the women of... loose morals flock."

"Oh, dear." Maggie continued to fan her face while anger rose through her body. The last thing she wanted to do was engage in a verbal sparring session with the area's most influential dragon, but the barb cut.

"I demand an explanation, Lady Parker." The ostrich feather on Lady Underhill's hat quivered in time to her extra flesh.

"Perhaps I may be of assistance." Stephen stepped forward from the milling crowd.

"Stephen." Maggie forgot herself at his appearance and breathed his name. A collective gasp swept through those people still assembled. She dropped the hand holding the fan as she gazed upon him. His cravat hung loose, and his hair was mussed as if he'd run his fingers through it. Her fingers itched to comb it back into place. "Please don't. You'll make it worse."

"Oh, I heartily doubt that. It would seem the *on dit* is correct in that you're a difficult woman to tame." His grin sent a different sort of heat through her limbs just before he focused on the dragon. "Lady Underhill, is it?" When she nodded, he took one of her gloved, bejeweled hands and pressed a kiss to the back of it. "I am Mr. Stephen Tarkington. May I explain my purpose in this debacle?"

"I suppose that would be all right." She simpered under his regard as if she were a young girl. "If Miss Manning is to be believed, you are a central part of the problem."

Stephen nodded. "Yes, Lady Parker and I were together this afternoon, but it's not unreasonable for a couple recently engaged to allow passion to sweep them away."

Surprised gasps filtered from the people still milling about the foyer, followed by calm so thick it seemed almost deafening.

Another wave of shock plowed through Maggie's insides. What was the man about? She employed her fan, frantically moving her hand while heat suffused her face. Her stays cut into her ribcage. *I cannot breathe.* Neither could she talk, so she waited for his next words.

Stephen released Lady Underhill's hand. "Oh, yes, shocking isn't it?" He nodded. "You should be proud that Lady Parker is making an honest man out of me. Where is the crime, I ask you?" He spun around to face the throng. "If anyone is to blame, it's me. I've been told I'm a charming, persuasive man." A few in the crowd mirrored his soft chuckle. "But, I *am* a gentleman, and I am prepared to make the situation right. I'll do whatever it takes to save my lady's reputation."

Maggie moved down another step. Her stomach knotted. Her heart beat a crazy rhythm. Why would he tell such an obvious falsehood? Did fondness for her motivate the speech or was this his way of securing financial backing into Parliament? She forced a swallow, but it didn't alleviate her dry throat. Why did she feel like laughing and crying by turns?

Her brother stepped to the front of the assemblage before Maggie could utter a word in her own defense. "I believe what Mr. Tarkington says is true." He clapped Stephen's shoulder. "I had cause to play matchmaker for the two, and have witnessed the genuine affection Stephen has for my sister." He glanced at Maggie, his expression a mix of honesty and apology. "I suspect she feels the same for him, if she'll let herself trust."

"Really, Alfie, you conspired with him?" Maggie clutched the stair rail, not quite willing to believe anything she'd heard this night.

A flush colored her brother's face. He adjusted his spectacles. "What can I say, Mags? If there are any two people who'd suit, it's you and him. Mark my words." He grinned and nodded at Stephen. "I'll track Amanda down and open the dancing. I think you and my sister have some things to sort through."

"We do. Thank you, Alfred." Stephen peered at Lady Underhill. "Will there be further objections?" His tone brooked no argument. "I fear I have a rather full schedule ahead."

"No, but I'll be watching you both." She sniffed and sailed into the crowd.

As the crowd realized the scandalous portion of the evening had concluded, they disbursed leaving Stephen in the foyer and Maggie on the stairs.

She stared at him as he walked to the foot of the staircase. Though his expression remained closed, his eyes, dear heaven his eyes, brimmed with pleading and a desire that stole her breath. "Why would you do this? You've landed us both in the soup for no reason." She couldn't decide if she wanted to rush down the stairs to smack him for his stupidity or hug him for his defense. Whatever had motivated it, he hadn't left her to the wolves.

"What can I say? You've had a profound effect on me." He laid a gloved hand on the railing and planted a foot on the stair.

In the end, curiosity won out above all else. "*Are* we truly engaged?"

"I would not have mentioned it if I didn't mean it, Maggie." His voice, so smoky and smooth, slid over her skin, and her heart fluttered.

She cleared her throat. "You said marriage didn't agree with you."

"Can I not change my mind? With the right woman, I believe I will have much different results. You are that woman."

"We've known each other scarcely a week."

"Ah, but what a great week it has been." One of his dark eyebrows inched upward. "Wouldn't you say?"

"Yes." Her spine tingled while mirroring tremors tickled her core. Maggie squeezed her thighs together. Why did he have to be so potent? "How can we know if a union will last a lifetime? If I marry again, I want it to be forever."

Stephen shrugged. "We don't, but we'll never know unless we try. Even you can't argue that we're well-matched. We're stubborn, persuasive, passionate, and determined."

"We are." Maggie grinned then berated herself for falling victim to his charm. "I'd have to forfeit my freedom."

"Not necessarily. Your sense of self-assurance is what initially attracted me to you. In fact," he came up one step, "I'd be content to let you do whatever you damn well please because you'll be mine. Spending a lifetime at your side is my prize; it matters not how we live it."

Maggie didn't want to melt from mere words, yet her knees threatened to buckle, and her legs trembled. She moved down another step. "I don't know what to say. It's a shock, of course, but in the end, it all depends on trust. Can I trust you, Stephen?" She and he shared nothing outside an affinity for carnal entertainment and mourning spouses and children. Would that be enough?

"Maggie, please." He advanced another step. "I know much of my past, as well as yours, is a mystery. What we do know and share is a good thing; it's more than many couples have, but that's part of the excitement. The ability to share secrets and truths is what keeps a marriage strong." A touch of desperation lined his face. "Think of it as an adventure, except this time you'll be having it with someone you admire and get on well with."

Tears crowded her throat. Her stomach shook with nerves she'd not known since she first came to England with her late husband. Could she take such an enormous chance? Should she? She'd known a spot of loneliness before the advent of Stephen. Was he what she needed to enhance her life? Maggie clutched the fan tighter. The fact that Alfie had given his support meant a great deal. Alfred's endorsements were never wrong.

"For the love of God, Maggie, say something, so I might know my fate." His voice rasped with emotion she'd previously not heard from him.

She took a few bracing breaths. Did her quest to do what she pleased outweigh her need for him? Her gaze landed on him, and she smiled. *Poor fellow.* He really did appear to have gone through the wringer. Yet throwing her lot in with Stephen promised adventure, and more scandal than she could ever dream of. Finally, not able to stand the tension between them or the emotions ravaging her mind, she shook her head. "I need some air."

Maggie gathered a handful of her skirts and rushed down the staircase and past Stephen to the front door. Caruthers scrambled ahead of her and had barely opened it before she ran through and out into the night. Chilly air enveloped her as she continued down the front steps and kept running along a dainty path lined with flowerbeds that would eventually lead to the side garden.

"Maggie, stop!" Stephen's command rang on the clear night, shortly followed by urgent footsteps. "Good God, woman, I never thought I'd see the day when you ran from your problems." He caught her up just as she slipped around the east side of the manor house, his eyes glittering in the dim light, his breathing ragged.

"I'm not running from them. I simply wished for a bit of privacy." Her heart thundered in her ears, and she leaned her back against the ivy-covered brick façade of the house. "And air.

I felt as if I'd burn to death in there, but these blasted stays..." She knew she owed him an answer, desperately wanted to give him the one sitting at the tip of her tongue, but niggling doubts kept her confirmation at bay. "Please tell me you didn't put forth this stunt as a way into politics. I cannot bear it if that's what prompted your declaration."

"No. If you've not believed anything else I've said to you, believe this." He rubbed a hand along his jaw. "Hell, if you don't believe me, that won't stop me. We'll live outside the bounds of proper society as long as I can be with you."

His earnest plea brought tears to her eyes. "I do love it when a man is desperate."

"Oh, I am." Stephen crept closer until he was separated from her by two feet. "Also, I didn't say those things to extricate us from a bramble." He bowed his head. "First and foremost, I never laid a finger on Amanda. I want that to be very clear. Yes, my original plan of wanting to court her was ill-advised, but all of that flew out of my head the moment I met you."

This was true. His intent had shifted as soon as she took him to task in the rose arbor. "I admit our meeting was unorthodox and highly scandalous." The remembrance of his caress that afternoon sent gooseflesh sailing over her skin.

Stephen's low laughter carried a note of triumph. He closed the distance between them and planted a hand on either side of her head, pinning her body between his and the wall of the house. "Give me a chance, Maggie. I'm but a man whose world has been turned upside down by an insatiable, highly improper woman. I want to be a better man for you." He paused, his jaw working. "Your fierce independence, the way you embrace life, the vulnerability you show when you think no one is looking, it's all quite heady. I want to share that and everything else with you."

She tried, oh how hard she tried, to ignore the warmth of his breath as it feathered along her cheek. She attempted to disregard how good the lean length of his body felt pressed against hers, but she wasn't strong enough. She craved his touch, his kiss. Hang it all, she wanted him, bad and good, every bit in between, every story that had created him, all that and more.

"You live and work in London. My life is here." It was her last holdout, but she had her pride, after all. Let him work a tad harder to win her.

"In the grand scheme, London isn't that far from Cranleigh, my dear, and besides, you've committed to accompanying Amanda to Town for the Season." He pressed closer, and his breath fanned her lips. "You wouldn't want to disappoint your niece, would you? Undoubtedly, we will be thrown together more often than not. Plenty of time for a courtship to play out while the banns are read and to complete any other paperwork or secure blessings from the Church we need."

Dear heavens, the banns. He is serious. "For Amanda's role in this scandal, I'll let her think she's going home." Maggie brought up her free hand and cupped his cheek. "She'll need to work for my good humor if she wants the London trip."

He inhaled sharply. "Does this mean you'll make me the happiest of men?"

"With marriage? You don't care for it."

Stephen turned his head and kissed her palm. "I suspect that was because I didn't know how to make a woman happy.

However, being leg-shackled to you will be the sweetest torture, and one I gladly look forward to. I know how to please you."

She finger-combed his hair into some semblance of order. "You won't care if I choose to swim naked or challenge the youths to horse races?"

"Not a whit." He nipped a line of feather-weighted kisses along the inside of her arm, but the glove prevented her from feeling the full effect. "In fact, I'll endeavor to join you, at least where the swimming is concerned, especially if a dalliance under the willows is the reward."

A shiver raced down her spine. Oh, the fun they'd have together! "I cannot promise you I'll be the ideal wife Society demands." Nor did she want to be that woman again. This marriage would be on her terms and for her enjoyment.

"I cannot promise you I won't be a rogue and goad you into being a wife far removed from those ideals Society paints. I am, after all, something of an outcast myself. In the end, it's what makes you unique, and quite the catch." He slipped an arm around her waist and pulled her flush against him. The brush of his erect cock left little doubt how much he desired her. "Will there be many more excuses? I've wanted to kiss you since you made your appearance this evening, and I only have so much patience."

"None that I can think of."

"You are a vision of loveliness in that gown. I cannot wait to take it off you."

"Oh, Stephen..." She'd barely uttered the words before he crushed his lips to hers.

Maggie surrendered to his embrace with a soft sigh. The strong bands of his arms around her lent her strength and she knew he'd protect her, defend her with his life if she asked. She dropped her fan, threw her arms around his neck and applied herself to the kiss with every ounce of feeling she'd held back since the affair began. His lips, firm and warm, moved over hers with purpose, and when the satin glide of his tongue along the seam of her mouth prompted her to open, she met each stroke, each fencing caress, with one of her own. An urgent throbbing plagued her core and dampness tickled the curls between her thighs. Heaven help her, but she needed him in her bed, this instant, regardless of the ball in progress.

This man of hers, she wanted him forever; she desired to be a better woman for him. Stephen had been correct; they were well-matched in every way that counted.

Languid heat surrounded her, consumed her limbs and flowed through her until she feared her legs wouldn't support her. Breaking the kiss, she pulled from his embrace. Her chest heaved as she sucked air into her corseted lungs. "Make love to me."

"Now?"

"Yes, right now. Here. We'll be hidden enough. Besides, I rather doubt anyone would look for us, not while Amanda is still likely seething at the refreshment table." Maggie grabbed his hand and tugged him deeper into the shrubbery crowding the side of the house. "Please."

"Maggie, love, are you sure?" His strong fingers closed around hers.

"Oh yes." She glanced at him. Her heart stuttered at the abject desire and the glimmer of love in his eyes. "I don't ever want to have you say to me later that I crumbled under convention and seduced you into a bed."

His surprised burst of laughter reverberated in her chest. "You, conventional? Not bloody likely." He wrapped his arms around her, turned them both and pressed her back against the wall while the tall shrubbery became a living shield.

"I'm glad you agree." The pungent scent of pine and growing things wafted into her nose. Being in his arms, resting in his masculine strength and knowing he belonged to her sent a feeling of peace over her. Her giggle was a throaty affair as she drew a hand between them to fumble at the fastenings of his trousers. "Imagine the scandal if we should be found."

"Somehow, my dear, I think each day with you will have potential for scandal, and I look forward to every minute of it." He batted her hand away in favor of manipulating the buttons himself. "If you hadn't agreed to the engagement, you still have made me the happiest of men."

"How do you figure?" As she helped him shuck down his trousers and short pants, her breasts grazed the front of his evening jacket and her nipples pebbled. The fine lawn of her shift abraded the sensitized tips, adding to her need. Oh, how she wanted to have his hands on her body and feel his cock inside her as he slid in and out.

"I never knew what I'd been missing in my life until I met you." He captured her lips with his. He drew long, drugging kisses from her, playing her mouth as if she were an instrument and he the master musician. When he finally allowed her breath, he said, "You've given me back the ability to laugh and to believe life is more than work and goals. It's chasing the unexpected for the thrill and the fun."

Maggie nodded, still fuzzy from his assault on her mouth. She moved a hand to cup his manhood and squeezed. His cock twitched in her palm. God, he felt so good. She curled her fingers around his shaft and drew her hand up and down his length. With every pass he thickened and filled her hand with hot, throbbing flesh. His groan made her grin. "There is one thing you must understand."

"Can I implore you to make it quick? I'd rather spend inside you instead of on your gown." Stephen gathered handfuls of her skirts and bunched them at her waist. "I can foresee many days and nights of our future filled with exploring positions in which to make love."

Liquid heat pooled between her thighs. "I intend to hold you to that promise." She squirmed against him as desire tightened her belly. "If I'm going to put an end to my grand affair by marrying you, you'd better take me with such force and enthusiasm that at the conclusion, I cannot envision my life without you in it."

"Then we are of an accord." He hooked a hand beneath one of her legs and pulled it over his hip. Maggie curled it around his waist while she clutched his shoulders, bringing him closer. "I shall endeavor to do my best."

She swallowed, but couldn't encourage moisture into her dry throat. The wide head of his cock bumped her swollen nubbin. She gasped as sensation shuddered and tingled through her breasts and core. "One more thing." The words rasped in the darkness. She'd break apart soon, yet this was important.

"Yes?" His voice was no less hoarse as if it took great effort to fight his body's urges.

She wriggled her hips. His cock slid down her wet folds to rest at her opening. Stephen grinned and gently entered her, paused, barely seated. Maggie groaned, but kept her focus on what she wanted to say. "I will sponsor your bid for a Parliament seat." She dug her fingers into his strong shoulders. "Beyond that, I intend to champion your cause and help you attain whatever goals you may have in your quest to change politics."

"Are you certain?"

"Yes." She nodded and then kissed his chin. "I give it to you freely and not from potential backlash from this evening's events. I want to see you succeed."

"Ah, how you humble me." Stephen rested his forehead against hers. "Thank you. I'll strive never to disappoint you."

Her heart stuttered at the wonder in his voice. "Marriage is a mutual endeavor. I'll help you, but in return I expect you to support me in whatever I do."

"Of course." He slid a hand to her bottom while shoving into her channel the rest of the way. "I look forward to the challenge."

"As do I." Her heartbeat accelerated and she wrapped her arms around his shoulders. Her inner muscles pulsed around his length in anticipation. "Unless..." She could barely form words while they were joined.

"Unless?" Stephen pulled out and his tip kissed her entrance, teasing, tormenting.

Maggie held his gaze in the darkness. Oh, this man would vex her and push her in all the ways that mattered. She couldn't wait for their future together. "Unless you fail to satisfy me tonight."

"You know not what you ask, love." His next thrust was powerful and filled her completely. "I intend to take that dare, because if I fail, I'll merely have to try again later."

She couldn't stop the shiver that wracked her body. A lifetime with Stephen, this vital, exciting, dedicated man. *I'm incredibly lucky.* In a roundabout way, she'd gotten her wish that a man would come to Surrey for her. Her heart swelled with the beginnings of love. "I agree." She shifted her hips and took him in even deeper. A host of tingles circled through her lower belly. "Now, please, finish me. I'm in desperate need."

"We cannot have that." He held her leg at his waist as he withdrew then slammed back into her. "I apologize in advance if this is quick."

Maggie was beyond caring. He was in her arms and moving within her body. For the moment, life was perfect. She met his thrusts as best she could in such a scandalous position. Gentle, steady, forceful, Stephen set a rhythm that had her head spinning and her core trembling. He squeezed her bottom and pressed her closer. Pressure bore down with urgent heat, and though every thrust brought her nearer to the edge, she craved release.

"I'm nearly gone." Stephen's efforts became frantic.

She slid a hand between them and fought through the cloud of skirting until her fingers glided over her swollen nubbin. Sensation engulfed her as she circled the button, faster, in time to Stephen's thrusts. His cock glided in and out. He filled her, hit every pleasure spot. Her eyes fluttered closed in bliss. One more strum over her flesh and she exploded. At her inhalation to scream, he claimed her mouth and took the shout into himself.

Her inner muscles clenched and spasmed around his pumping shaft. Her legs trembled. She held onto his shoulders as they were the only thing keeping her upright. The strength left her legs while bliss overtook her. Stephen grunted. He raised his head and thrust once more. The warm stream of his seed shot into her core then he sagged against her, pressing her back into the wall of the manor.

Oh, yes, he would do nicely.

"That wasn't bad, but next time—" She relaxed her leg and unwrapped it from his body.

He cut her off with a quick kiss and then pulled out. Immediately, she missed that heated connection. "Next time, we will copulate in a proper bed, but I'll concede and let you choose the position. After all, there must be some compromise between us."

Was there any wonder why she adored him?

Her skirts drifted back into place. "Cheeky man. It would seem your desire for scandal equals mine."

And it was what she'd always chased throughout her adult life.

She burrowed into his embrace, content to remain there and listen to the thundering beat of his heart. Never had she anticipated that her quest for an affair would bring her the very man she never knew she needed.

The End

Find the continuing adventures of Maggie and Stephen in...

Library Tryst

It's been a month since Maggie, Lady Parker, met Stephen Tarkington then proceeded to tumble headlong into scandal. On the evening of a dinner party, she's vexed due to a misplaced fan. Though she's madly in love with her fiancé, she's been too busy to be with him as much as she'd like.

Stephen adores Maggie. He can't wait until they're joined in wedded bliss and has just the thing to calm nerves frazzled from wedding planning and playing hostess—a library tryst. He steals her fan then entices her into the room a mere hour before her guests are due to arrive.

Erotic delights occur once clothing is shed and kisses land in places that are rather scandalous and entirely satisfying.

Warning: at 5K words, this is a short story. For longer novels, please browse the *Scandal in Surrey* collection.

Regency-era romances by Sandra Sookoo

Colors of Scandal series

Dressed in White
Draped in Green
Trimmed in Blue
Wrapped in Red
Graced in Scarlet
Adorned in Violet
Embellished in Mauve
Clad in Midnight
Garbed in Purple
Resplendent in Ruby
Cloaked in Shadows
Decorated in Christmas
Tangled in Lavender
Persuasive in Pink
Disguised in Tartan (coming April 2022)
Attired in Highland Gold (coming April 2022)
Hopeful in Yellow (coming August 2022)
Imperfect in Peridot (coming October 2022)
Christmas in Crimson (coming November 2022)

Storme Brothers series

The Soul of a Storme
The Heart of a Storme
The Look of a Storme
A Storme's Christmas Legacy
A Storme's First Noelle (in the *Star of Light* anthology)
The Sting of a Storme
The Touch of a Storme
The Fury of a Storme (coming May 2022)

Home for the Holidays series

The Folly of Caroling

Three Mistletoe Kisses
Silver Bells Scandal
A Holly and Ivy Affair
Lords of the Night series
Devil Take the Duke
Bitten by the Earl
Adrift with the Viscount
Treasured by the Earl
Transformed by a Christmas Star
Pistols at Dawn, Your Grace, as part of the *Shifting Hearts* boxed set
Willful Winterbournes series
Romancing Miss Quill (coming June 2022)
Pursuing Mr. Mattingly (coming August 2022)
Courting Lady Yeardly (coming October 2022)
Teasing Miss Atherby (coming late 2022 or early 2023?)
Singular Sensation series
One Little Indiscretion (coming July 2022)
One Secret Wish (coming September 2022)
One Tiny On-Dit Later (coming January 2023)
One Accidental Night with an Improper Duke (coming March 2023)
One Scandalous Choice (coming May 2023)
One Thing Led to Another (coming July 2023)
One Too Many Suitors (coming September 2023)
One Thing Led to Another (November 2023)
Mary and Bright series
A Mary and Bright Christmastide (coming December 2023)
A Springtime Engagement (TBA)
An Autumnal Partnership (TBA)
Diamonds of London series
My Dear Mr. Ridley (coming February 14, 2023)
The Clever Widow's Wager (coming April 23, 2023)
Catch Her if You Can (coming June 13, 2023)
Yours Respectfully, My Lord (coming August 15, 2023)
When the Duke Said Yes (coming September 14, 2023)
To Love a Ghostly Lord (coming October 17, 2023)
One Hell of a Christmas (coming November 20, 2023)

Along Came Tess (coming January 16, 2024)
The Duke's Valentine (coming February 13, 2024
Not in His Usual Style (coming March 12, 2024)
The Merry Month of May (coming April 16, 2024)
The Duchess Problem (coming May 14, 2024)
Spirited Away by the Viscount (June 11, 2024)

Thieves of the Ton series
Captivated by an Adventurous Lady
Engaged to a Scandalous Earl
Married on a Wicked Morning
Intrigued by an Ancient Pedigree
Beguiled on a Christmas Morning: Christmas novella
Caught with a Stolen Diamond
Tortured by a Horrible Secret
Delighted on a Summer's Evening
Trapped in the British Museum
Charmed at a Yuletide Ball
One Silent Night
Redeeming a Tarnished Lord
Lords of Happenstance series
What the Stubborn Viscount Desires
What a Wayward Lord Needs
What the Dashing Duke Deserves
Scandal in Surrey series
Lady Parker's Grand Affair
The Bride's Gambit
Misfortune's Lady
Miss Bennett's Naughty Secret
Standalone Regency romances
Lady Isabella's Splendid Folly
Wagering on Christmas
Magic in Mayflowers
Act of Pardon

Angel's Master
Storm Tossed Rogue
Claiming His Wife
Scoundrel's Trespass
On a Midnight Clear
A Fowl Christmastide
His Pretend Duchess
Visions of Christmastide
An Accidental Countess
A Rogue for Lady Peacock (coming September 2022)
The Most Wonderful Earl of the Year (coming November 2022)
Snowflakes for the Earl (coming December 2022)
She's Got a Duke to Keep Her Warm (coming December 2022)
The Most Wonderful Earl of the Year (coming December 2022)
The Lyon's Dilemma (Lyon's Den connected world) (coming January 2023)

Author Bio

Sandra Sookoo is a *USA Today* bestselling author who firmly believes every person deserves acceptance and a happy ending. Most days you can find her creating scandal and mischief in the Regency-era, serendipity and happenstance in Victorian America or snarky, sweet humor in the contemporary world. Most recently she's moved into infusing her books with mystery and intrigue. Reading is a lot like eating fine chocolates—you can't just have one. Good thing books don't have calories!

When she's not wearing out computer keyboards, Sandra spends time with her real-life Prince Charming in central Indiana where she's been known to goof off and make moments count because the key to life is laughter. A Disney fan since the age of ten, when her soul gets bogged down and her imagination flags, a trip to Walt Disney World is in order. Nothing fuels her dreams more than the land of eternal happy endings, hope and love stories.

Stay in Touch

Sign up for Sandra's bi-monthly newsletter and you'll be given exclusive excerpts, cover reveals before the general public as well as opportunities to enter contests you won't find anywhere else.

Just send an email to sandrasookoo@yahoo.com with SUBSCRIBE in the subject line.

Or follow/friend her on social media:

Facebook: https://www.facebook.com/sandra.sookoo

Facebook Author Page: https://www.facebook.com/sandrasookooauthor/

Pinterest: https://www.pinterest.com/sandrasookoo/

Instagram: https://www.instagram.com/sandrasookoo/

BookBub Page: https://www.bookbub.com/authors/sandra-sookoo

Don't miss out!

Visit the website below and you can sign up to receive emails whenever Sandra Sookoo publishes a new book. There's no charge and no obligation.

https://books2read.com/r/B-A-PDBB-CQIE

BOOKS 2 READ

Connecting independent readers to independent writers.

9 798201 205195